Kink

Kink

SASKIA WALKERAND**SASHA WHITE**

HEAT | NEW YORK

THE BERKLEY PUBLISHING GROUP
Published by the Penguin Group
Penguin Group (USA) Inc.
375 Hudson Street, New York, New York 10014, USA
Penguin Group (Canada), 90 Eglinton Avenue East, Suite 700, Toronto, Ontario, M4P 2Y3, Canada
(a division of Pearson Penguin Canada Inc.)
Penguin Books Ltd., 80 Strand, London WC2R 0RL, England
Penguin Group Ireland, 25 St. Stephen's Green, Dublin 2, Ireland (a division of Penguin Books Ltd.)
Penguin Group (Australia), 250 Camberwell Road, Camberwell, Victoria 3124, Australia
(a division of Pearson Australia Group Pty. Ltd.)
Penguin Books India Pvt. Ltd., 11 Community Centre, Panchsheel Park, New Delhi—110 017, India
Penguin Group (NZ), Cnr. Airborne and Rosedale Roads, Albany, Auckland 1310, New Zealand
(a division of Pearson New Zealand Ltd.)
Penguin Books (South Africa) (Pty.) Ltd., 24 Sturdee Avenue, Rosebank, Johannesburg 2196,
South Africa

Penguin Books Ltd., Registered Offices: 80 Strand, London WC2R 0RL, England

This book is an original publication of The Berkley Publishing Group.

This is a work of fiction. Names, characters, places, and incidents either are the product of the authors' imagination or are used fictitiously, and any resemblance to actual persons, living or dead, business establishments, events, or locales is entirely coincidental. The publisher does not have any control over and does not assume any responsibility for author or third-party websites or their content.

First edition: February 2007

Library of Congress Cataloging-in-Publication Data

Kink / Saskia Walker and Sasha White.—1st ed.
     p.   cm.
   ISBN-13: 978-0-425-21399-5
   1. Erotic stories, American. I. White, Sasha, 1969– Watch me. II. Walker, Saskia, Sex, lies, and bondage tape.
   PS648.E7K56   2007
   813.'60803538—dc22   2006028099

PRINTED IN THE UNITED STATES OF AMERICA

10 9 8 7 6 5 4 3 2 1

Contents

Sex, Lies, and
Bondage Tape

SASKIA WALKER

**For Mark,
my real life hero**

Acknowledgments

I am indebted to my dear friends Michael Johnson, Banquo, and Matt North, for background information for this novella. Michael introduced me to the music promotions business, teaching me much about the other side of live performance and backstage antics. Banquo and Matt introduced me to the dedicated life of a musician, showing me how a studio works and giving me a true flavor of the lifestyle. I'm also indebted to Al Spicer, who encouraged my music writing, and published several of my pieces in the *Penguin Rough Guide to Rock*. Guys, you gave me the confidence and knowledge to set stories in the music world. Thank you.

ChapterOne

The atmosphere in the auditorium was electric. High on adrenaline-fueled energy, the crowd was humming with expectancy. Kelly Burton felt powerful, her body more than ready to rock some more. It was an outstanding concert, the last of a long European tour, and there was still more music to come. She squeezed her friend Helen's arm. "Ready for the final encore?"

Helen nodded. "I hope he does 'Squandered.' It's my favorite."

Before Kelly had a chance to answer, the stage lights dipped, swung skyward, and then beamed back onto the stage, delivering a sequence of red and purple pools of light that synchronized to the beat of the drums. A cheer went up from the crowd as Clayton Warren—aka rock god of the moment—walked back on stage. He lifted his hands, acknowledging the cheers and the sound of feet thumping on the floor. He was a London man, so this was a home-coming gig.

"Oh, give me strength, he's taken off his shirt," Helen shouted over the noise, grabbing a quick photo on her phone. "Jojo is going to be so sorry she missed this."

Kelly nodded and chuckled, pushing her damp hair back from her forehead, jostling with the crowd who pressed up against them, ready to rock. The audience roared when Clayton picked up his guitar, showing its appreciation for the sexy man on stage. The crowd was mixed, from serious rock fans to lusting women of all ages. Squealing teens and mature housewives stood side by side, ogling him. Kelly couldn't help admiring him too, even though she'd only come to the concert because her friend Jojo was having her leg pinned back together after a skiing accident. Jojo and Helen, her housemates, were the hardcore fans. It didn't stop Kelly from enjoying the music and appreciating a fine male body when she saw it, though. And it was fine.

Lean but muscled, his torso glistened with sweat, his long, damp hair flashing out as he moved. He stroked one hand down the neck of his guitar in the most deliberately suggestive way, which drew another cheer from the audience. He grinned, white teeth gleaming. Clayton Warren was a true performer.

The backing guitarist and bass player took their places. The drummer led them into the intro of the track, then Clayton let it rip. Running forward on the stage, he dropped to his knees in the spotlight, his body arched back as he delivered the distinctive riff of "Squandered," his top-selling single, still on the rock charts after four solid months.

The crowd surged in unison, arms waving, bodies moving to the rhythm of the song. Kelly moved with them, her energy level soaring. The song was a real rock anthem, and although she was enjoying it, her mind was also operating on a different plane. After a few moments, she leaned over to Helen and spoke into her ear.

"I'm going to go backstage." She pointed over to a curtained passageway on the side of the stage, where a couple of security men stood watching the gig. "Going to try to get an autograph for Jojo." She'd been turning the idea over in her mind during the second half of the concert and had decided to act on her plan.

Helen shook her head but grinned. "You're crazy, you'll never get past security."

"You know me. Never say, never." The two of them worked together running a health and fitness club, where Kelly was known as "the woman on a mission." "I'll meet you out front afterward. Keep your phone switched on, in case we can't find each other."

Helen nodded.

Kelly gave her two thumbs-up, and then ducked into the crowd. It was tightly packed and she had to squeeze and wheedle her way through it. More than ever she was glad of her skimpy halter-neck top. The auditorium was steaming and it was a genuine workout just being there.

Once she reached the area where the crowd thinned out at the side of the venue, and people were resting up against the walls, she headed down toward the curtained entrance to the backstage area. She paused a few feet away, watching the stage with one eye and the security men with the other. There were two uniformed officials who looked like they worked for the venue, and with them, a third man. He was wearing jeans and a black leather jacket.

The third man was built, at least as impressive as the two security guards, if not more so. Because Kelly worked in a gym she noticed these things. A fit man always inspired her interest. His dark blond hair made her want to run her fingers through it. It was thick and hung below his ears. One of the security guards said something to him and he laughed, moving briefly into the light. He had a great smile, and for a moment she almost forgot her mission. Jojo was sitting at home injured, moping with a glass of wine and playing her Clayton Warren CDs. The least Kelly could do was try to bring her a souvenir.

She sidled along the wall, watching the curtain moving on the currents of air passing through the auditorium. When one of the security men turned to look in her direction, she leaned against the wall and clapped along to the music. When he glanced away, she darted to the near end of the curtain. Lifting it, she disappeared behind it.

Her heart raced as she got her bearings. She'd made it backstage. At the end of a narrow corridor, a staircase led down. The dressing rooms had to be under the stage. There was nowhere else to go; this had to be the way. Elation hit her as she descended the stairs. She started mentally humming the *Mission Impossible* theme.

Glancing in both directions, she saw what looked like dressing rooms lined up to her right and darted that way, reading the numbers on the doors as she passed. Clayton would be designated Room One, surely? At the other end of the corridor, she saw another staircase. That had to be the way to the stage. Behind her, she heard voices.

"Did you see someone make it through?" a voice shouted.

Had one of the security men spotted her after all? She really oughtn't to be down here, but an urge to live dangerously had her firmly in its grip. She hurried on, gratified to see the numbers descending as she passed the doors. The door to Room Two was ajar, voices and laughter emerging from inside. She slowed down and walked past, glancing in with a nonchalant smile. Two or three members of the opening band were in there, busy with the press and beer.

When she got to the room marked One, she paused and put her ear to the door. All quiet. It could be the place, or it could be the manager's office for all she knew. Footsteps echoed down the stairway behind her. Turning the handle, she stepped inside, trying to gauge whether it was Clayton's dressing room. A rail of clothes stood in one corner. On the other side a dressing table was strewn with makeup equipment, glasses, and a half-empty bottle of champagne. The room smelled of expensive male cologne.

Above her, the ceiling thumped with bass-driven rock. The encore was in its final throes. A second shout echoed down the corridor outside. Definitely security, but now that she was in here there was no going back—besides, she hadn't come this far to miss her opportunity. Darting into the dark corner behind the clothes rail, she decided to hide until the security man was gone.

The door opened. Peeking between the clothes on the rail, she saw that it was the attractive bloke in the leather jacket; he was scanning the room. He had to be a roadie; he knew his way around back here. Once again, she couldn't help admiring him. He was striking in looks as well as physique.

His glance zoomed to where she stood. Pressing back into the darkness, she shut her eyes and held her breath. A moment later, she heard voices and footsteps echoing away. When she opened her eyes and exhaled, she saw that the door was still ajar. The music upstairs had stopped. Noise was gathering in the corridor outside. Her chance to get Clayton's autograph and put a smile on Jojo's face was on its way. When the door was pushed wide open and Clayton himself entered, her mood was triumphant.

He paced across the room towards her hiding place, bouncing on the balls of his feet as he walked, obviously wired from his performance. His hair was pushed back over his head, damp and clinging to his skull, his leather pants molded to his warm body. She could see the sweat glistening on his naked torso. She bit her lip, smiling to herself—if Jojo could see him now she'd have an orgasm on the spot. He looked hot, although personally Kelly preferred men with more meat on their bones.

So far so good. She was in the right place to get an autograph, but she hadn't envisaged being behind a clothes rail at this point. She was about to cough and emerge from the hiding place when people spilled into the room behind Clayton, a couple of the musicians and others, men and women. *Oh, joy.* She hadn't figured there would be so many extras in the entourage. This could make getting Jojo's autograph complicated, unless, of course, she could just merge in among them.

One bloke seemed to be taking charge, pushing the small crowd back out into the corridor. "Listen up, everyone," he shouted. "Clayton needs a little time to shower and change before we party." A cheer went up when he mentioned the word *party*. "Head upstairs to the hospitality suite and follow the corridor behind the stage. Give him ten minutes and he'll be right there."

The man was tall but lean like Clayton, his limber body perfectly outlined in faded jeans and a khaki-colored T-shirt. When he'd convinced all the hangers-on to get out, he shut the door and looked back over at Clayton. Clayton was still facing Kelly's way but he was smiling, as if he knew what was going on behind him. "Nice job, Jay," he commented.

The other man walked over and stood close behind him. "That's what I'm here for."

Clayton's grin grew. "Is it?"

Kelly's eyebrows lifted, realization hitting her. She was now stuck in a very personal moment. As if to prove the point, the man named Jay put one possessive arm around Clayton's bare chest, locking in behind him, his mouth descending to Clayton's shoulder.

Kelly watched in amazement as the man bared his teeth and bit into Clayton's shoulder. Clayton wasn't complaining though. In fact, when the other bloke's hand moved down to his belt, he shut his eyes and groaned aloud. The sound was definitely one of pleasure, sexual. *Clayton Warren is gay?* Clayton's hand locked over Jay's, forcing it lower, into the zipper area. He definitely wasn't fighting the other bloke off.

She tried not to look but couldn't help herself. The image of the two men locked together like that was so hot. She was riveted. Her pulse was pounding, her body humid. Her hair clung to her cheek, making her long to swipe it away.

Jay's hand moved to the button, then the zipper.

Oh my god. Kelly pressed back into the shadows. She was a mere three feet away from them, and they were so into each other they had no clue.

The sound of the zipper lowering was loud—hellishly loud—and slow, each tooth snapping free. Then Clayton's cock was out and being expertly handled by the other man. He smoothed his hand over it, drawing back the foreskin in even, practiced strokes.

Clayton's head dropped back, his body arched. His hips jutted forward and his mouth open, his teeth bared.

What a sight.

His cock was fully erect, a drop of semen gathering on its tip as Jay worked the shaft. He must have already been hard, in expectation of this after-show treat.

Arousal soared through her, arousal and disbelief. How the hell had she gotten herself into this? She swore silently, ruing her urge to go autograph-hunting. She'd now gotten herself stuck in a live man-on-man sex show and was privy to one of the best-kept secrets in the rock world. Despite all the press coverage featuring him and numerous attractive women, pinup boy Clayton Warren had a male lover. And right now she had an eyeful of their intimate behavior.

"Oh yeah, I need this," Clayton grunted. His cock was rigid, the head dark with blood, stretched to its limits, fit to burst.

She pressed back against the wall. *How do I get out of here?* There was a knock at the door and it opened. Hope leapt inside her.

"Sorry, Clayton," a voice declared, "but I think we've got a groupie on the loose."

A groupie? They had to be talking about her. Her heart sank to her boots. *Jesus, could this get any worse?*

Jay moved away from Clayton, turning toward the voice.

Over Clayton's shoulder, she could see the attractive security bloke give a reassuring nod to Jay.

"I'm on the case, but I thought Clayton would rather know."

"Sure thing, Tommy," Clayton replied through tense lips, hauling his zipper shut.

With no small effort, Kelly noticed. Forcing that meaty erection undercover was inevitably going to be a tough job. He looked positively exasperated, and who could blame him?

Sweat had now gathered in her cleavage. The combination of arousal and agitation was causing chaos inside her, threatening to unhinge her. She wanted to bolt for the door, push past the big bloke, and make a run for it. The remaining bit of sense she owned told her that would be the wrong thing to do.

A moment later, the big bloke ducked out and Clayton stalked over to the dressing table. Jay joined him and she could hear reassuring murmurs, but Kelly's attention was now focused on something else entirely—the door to the corridor had been left open. Could she make it?

Clayton and Jay were facing away, which would give her a head start. *Go girl, you can do it.* She counted to three, took a deep breath, and then crept out of her hole. Squeezing through the clothes, she tiptoed across the floor. Gathering speed as she got to the door, she grabbed the doorframe, rounded the corner—and ran straight into a wall of muscle.

Stunned, her eyes shut and then opened, cautiously. Peeking upwards, she recognized the granite jaw of the security man in the leather jacket. *Oh joy, I've run straight into him.* One large, powerful hand clamped against her back, winding her as he locked her against him.

He gave a husky laugh, keeping her pinned close to him. "Not so fast, lady."

Looking up, she saw the stubble on his chin, his twinkling eyes, and the thick, dark blond hair that fell across his forehead. He was indeed a particularly fit-looking specimen of a man, even if he did have her trapped in a vise. Under different circumstances, she might have bought him a drink.

Coughing, she wriggled her crushed boobs free, trying to make a point. She was a bona fide ticket buyer; she couldn't be treated this way. Could she? She stomped her foot on the floor, the only part of her body that she could actually move. "Let me go, I only wanted an autograph for a friend."

"That's what they all say." He lifted her bodily, leaving her feet dangling. "Autographs are available through the fan site."

"But I—"

"Groupie hunt over," he bellowed along the corridor.

His voice rumbled through her chest, making her pulse race. Perplexed at the effect he had on her, she prodded him with the finger he had jammed against his pecs. "How dare you. I'm not a groupie."

He looked down at her with amusement, green eyes narrowed with interest. He had a wide smile, teasing.

"Nice job, Tommy boy." It was Clayton and he was behind her.

She glanced back and then peered up at the big bloke beseechingly, hoping he wouldn't reveal that she'd just shot out of Clayton's dressing room.

"Give her hell, Tommy," Jay's voice announced. "She's all yours, call it a perk of the job."

Kelly's jaw dropped. He couldn't mean it?

Without warning, the big man laughed, lifted her, and threw her over his shoulder.

Shocked, she clutched at the back of his jacket for balance, her world spinning. He had her in a fireman's lift and there was nothing she could do about it. Voices and laughter from farther down the corridor assured her that others were watching the whole embarrassing scene. Her boobs were spilling out of her top, her bottom sticking in the air for all to see. And yet . . . somehow the idea of being carried away by the big bloke got to her. *Sexually.* She heated through in a flash and then whimpered, clutching at his massive, muscled body through his clothing.

He stroked the back of her leather-clad thighs with one warm hand.

That felt good, really good, and the way he had her positioned, her leather hipsters were pulled tight into her pussy, driving her crazy. *Focus*, she told herself. You might be in an intensely physical and compromised situation, but be sensible and use your head.

"Okay, it was wrong of me to come down here," she admitted, waving one hand. "But I only wanted an autograph for a friend, an injured friend who couldn't make it. I didn't mean to do anything else, honestly."

"Oh, but you did. You were a naughty girl, and you'll be punished." He gave a rumbling laugh and then set off. His hands were locked tightly around the back of her thighs.

She swore aloud. Her boobs were almost out of her top now and she felt as if the whole world were looking at her. The corridor shifted in her vision and two pairs of feet came into view—presumably Clayton and Jay.

"You can't be serious," she pleaded, forcing her head up, looking at the two men who looked on with amusement as she was carried off like some primeval caveman's prize. "I don't deserve to be treated like this." That seemed to make them laugh even more. They had to be kidding. She was about to beg to be put down when she was smacked across the bottom by one large hand.

"Bad girl," her captor bellowed, chuckling to himself.

Any notion of using her head was lost in an instant. Heat leapt out from the spot he'd spanked, spreading across the top of her thighs and shooting deep, right to her core. Her heart missed a beat; she struggled for breath. She shuddered and moaned, her clit tingling with heat. Liquid fire poured out of her core and her body went boneless with lust, falling limp over his shoulder. She clutched at his jacket with trembling fingers, her mind echoing with the primitive call of instinctive need: *take me, use me, fill me*.

The crowd faded away, everything faded away as he carried her off down a corridor, where the light grew dim and all she was aware of was him—his massive presence and his control over her. *I want him*. Somewhere at the back of her mind the *Mission Impossible* theme started up again.

T ommy Sampson was surprised, to say the least. Usually by this point they were thumping and kicking and bemoaning the fact they were being taken away from their beloved Clayton. It was a familiar scenario, but this woman was making panting noises and wriggling around as if she were on the brink of an orgasm.

She was a sexy number too. When she'd run slap-bang into him and he'd grabbed ahold of her, he was instantly reminded of the cover of a *Modesty Blaise* novel that he'd kept by his bedside as a teenager. He'd liked the cover model who represented the sexy female secret agent, and had held on to the book for weeks after he'd finished reading it. He hadn't thought of it in years, but this woman had stimulated the memory. That wasn't all she had stimulated.

She looked good in those leather pants, and her breasts shifting against him under her skimpy top instantly made him think of sex. Right now heat was pouring off her in waves. She smelled good too—sexy—a mixture of perfume and hormones.

"You are in big trouble, madam. Nobody gets past me during the last encore." He gave her another spank as he walked down the corridor toward one of the hidden exits at the back of the building. He couldn't resist it.

She wriggled against him, making another dirty-sex noise. Yup, she was turned on, unmistakably turned on. He couldn't help smiling. Normally his he-man act sent them off in a rush of humiliation. He'd worked for Clayton during his tours for the last three years, and he'd gotten the act down to a fine art by the end of the first tour. With the real bad cases, the ones who got into the dressing rooms like this one had, Clayton played into it as well, which usually worked a treat for sending them on their way.

The corridor was dingy, the overhead lightbulb weak and flickering. He didn't really want to put her down at all, but they had reached the security door at the back of the building. The door opened on to a narrow alleyway, which led a convoluted path back onto the main street. He just had to enter the code into the keypad, and she could be on her merry way.

"Here you go, madam." He eased her down a fraction, so that she could straighten up in his grip, and then paused. He could have just put her feet down on the floor, but this was too much fun. He wanted to savor lowering her. Her body was toned under his hands, and he mused that she would make a great gym partner.

She was secure, but she clutched at him, her hands going to his shoulders as she straightened. She shook her hair back. Short and thick, it fell back into place around her head. Her face was flushed, her eyes glinting in the gloomy light. Her wide mouth was open, her lips damp. She looked like a cat about to pounce.

He paused, staring up at her. His spine stiffened, a dull ache at its base working its way into his consciousness. Unsurprisingly, he was getting hard. He had a whole lot of woman in his arms, after all, and she was looking good. Her breasts were just under his chin, her hips against his belly. It was a recipe for arousal.

She let out a soft laugh. "That was quite a ride." She arched one slim eyebrow.

"You weren't supposed to enjoy it, my dear." He couldn't restrain his grin.

She wriggled in his grasp, but clutched tighter. "I thought you might be enjoying it too." She bit her lip, an action that made her even more sexy looking.

"I am." Savoring each moment, he eased her down, his hands shifting around her hips. She definitely wasn't wearing a bra. Her nipples were hard inside that top of hers. When his hands reached her buttocks, he cupped them.

She moved her hands, latching her fingers around his head, and then—to his astonishment—she opened her legs and wrapped them around his hips.

She doesn't want you to put her down, bozo.

The fact hit him like a freight train, and then some other form of rationale took over: instinct. He turned, wedging her back against the closed door, jamming his hips between her open legs.

"What's the matter, afraid to let go?" he teased. He leaned into her hair, smelling her.

"I like it here." She leaned back against the door, pivoting against it and riding her pussy up and down against the growing erection inside his jeans.

He groaned.

"Do you have to rush off?" She had her hands in his hair and, as she moved them, she brushed the secret, sensitive spot below his left ear that sent him off the rails with lust. Blood rushed to his groin. His heart hammered in his chest, his hips rolled into hers.

"Rushing off anywhere isn't an option right now," he managed to mutter, and leaned into her neck, his mouth against her skin. He could feel her breath warm on his face. He traced a path with his mouth down toward her jaw.

Her head sank back in response.

He kissed the skin beneath her ear. She smelled of jasmine, and unmistakable desire. He could hear the withheld whimper in her throat; he could sense her reactions coursing over her skin. Her hands were on his shoulders, drawing him in. She was hot, responsive. She was everything that made his blood turn to fire and his lust palpable. He breathed his way to her jaw and then she turned her mouth into his, meeting him.

Her mouth was soft but active, an explosive combination. Her lips moved against his hungrily, then she opened her mouth, her tongue teasing his into her mouth.

He staggered, his grip on her buttocks failing.

She slid to the floor but clutched at him, not breaking the kiss.

His hands moved up and to her top. He felt her breathing grow shallow as he ran his hands over the outline of her breasts under the soft fabric.

She shivered, leaning back and looking up at him. Reaching

down and stroking her hand against his dick, she gave a husky laugh. "That's a good, solid package you've got there."

When she touched him like that, he couldn't think straight. "You're a bad girl."

"Does that mean you're going to spank me again?"

He groaned and pushed her against the door. "I think you deserve it, don't you?"

"Maybe you're right." A wild streak was visible in her expression.

"You like playing rough, do you?" Logic was gone; his dick had well and truly taken over his brain.

"You better believe it." She moved suddenly, stretching up to him, grazing his chin with her teeth. Her hands were measuring him up—back, shoulders, and biceps—while she kissed his neck. Her breasts, pert and high under her top, made his hands gravitate toward them.

He reached under it, his thumbs stroking her nipples until they were hard and jutting. He wanted to fuck her right there and then, up against the wall, rough and ready.

You vowed never to get involved with groupies, his conscience reminded him. *She wanted Clayton; you're just a convenient second choice for a woman in heat.* But she was all over him, so inviting, and his body was tuning his conscience out.

Her hands gripped his buttocks, digging into them roughly, pulling him closer.

He ground hard against her. He had condoms in his wallet, a three-pack. He wanted to use them all, in quick succession. The sudden sound of a mobile phone ringing interrupted that chain of thought, grounding him somewhat as he tried to work out where the sound was coming from.

She pulled her head back and raised one perfectly arched eyebrow. "Is that a vibrator in your pocket or are you just pleased to see me?"

When she laughed her nipples bounced, the hard little nubs poking through the fabric of her top, drawing his attention. He ran his thumbs over them, unable to resist.

"Oh I'm pleased to see you, but I think the vibrations are coming from your side." Probably a boyfriend or husband, he realized, waiting outside. He'd seen it before, women coming backstage while their boyfriends waited outside. It didn't make any sense to him. He eased away from her.

She fumbled for her hip pocket.

He had to ask. "Boyfriend?" He stepped back, giving her space.

"No, I'm single. What about you, have you got a boyfriend?" She laughed softly. "Or is that just Clayton's thing?"

Damn. He was hoping there hadn't been anything going on when she was in the dressing room. It had to happen eventually, he figured. Clayton and Jay's affair had been going on for months and they'd gotten away with it so far through sheer luck. "You saw them together?"

She pulled the phone out of her pocket. "I take it it's a secret?"

That sense of humor of hers was mischievous. He nodded. He was going to have to speak to her, talk her out of going to the press if it was at all possible. They weren't ready for that kind of exposure yet and might never be. Clayton had only confided in him because they needed his understanding and vigilance, but Clayton had also confided he was afraid the truth would ruin his career.

He reached over and punched the key code into the door, pushing it open to get some air. He needed to clear his head.

"I better get this, it's my housemate. I came to the gig with her and she's probably wondering where I am." She flicked the phone open and moved into the doorway, but kept one hand on his shoulder, maintaining the contact between them.

She'd said there was no boyfriend. It was a relief to find he hadn't just been mauling some other man's woman. He glanced over her. Her Doc Marten boots made him smile—she wasn't like the other groupies. He didn't seem to be clearing his head, after all. The more he looked at her, the more he wanted her.

"Hi, Helen. Yes, I'm fine." She sidled a glance over his torso as she spoke, as if weighing her thoughts and words carefully. Her hand moved inside his jacket, down and across his chest while her gaze held his.

The way she handled him so confidently made him want to throw her on her back and climb all over her. In fact, if she hadn't been talking on the phone, she'd be back up against the wall in a flash.

"No, I didn't get the autograph." She ran her hand over the bulge of his dick. "But something else just as exciting came up." She fixed him with a wicked stare.

Fuck, she's hot. He latched his hands around her hips, pulling her up against him, needing that warm shape of her groin against his dick again.

She leaned back in his grip, pivoting her hips against his, the expression in her eyes inviting him in. "Don't worry, I'm okay. I'm getting to know a new friend." Her free hand went up to his neck and she pulled him down for a quick kiss before continuing her conversation.

"Why don't you make your way home, and I'll catch up with

you there later on?" She laughed softly in response to whatever the woman on the other end of the phone said. "Oh, I will." Flapping the phone shut she pushed it back into that tight hip pocket of hers.

They watched each other silently a moment. She'd put her cards on the table; her words had been as much for him as her friend.

Voices passed by the end of the alleyway; she glanced after them, then back at him. The moonlight caught her expression. There was wildness in her eyes and it triggered something inside him. All thoughts of avoiding groupies were vanishing from his mind. She didn't have a boyfriend, that's all that *really* mattered. She wanted him, and she was hotter than hell. Besides, he could maybe talk her out of blabbing about Clayton, if he got her alone for a while. His mind was just about functioning enough to latch on to that reason to pursue her. His dick had its own agenda.

"My name is Kelly." She reached out for his hands. Drawing them toward her she put them back on her waist, where they'd been earlier.

"Tommy," he murmured, as he ran his hands under her top again, pushing it up. Her bare breasts in his hands compelled him to stroke and mold the soft, warm flesh.

"So, Tommy, do you have to get back to Clayton?" Her voice was a whisper, her eyelids lowering as his hands moved over her breasts.

"No, there's a party here on-site, my work is done." Her top was gathering on the back of his hands, he could see the soft undersides of her breasts and bent to suck her nipple through the fabric, partly to stop himself from exposing her completely.

She whimpered.

He growled.

"Shall we go somewhere?" She had one hand up against the doorframe to steady them both. "Because otherwise we might be charged with indecent exposure in a public thoroughfare."

He couldn't help laughing. She had a reckless way about her that was infectious. "Fast mover, aren't you?"

She shrugged. "Life is short."

She was so right. The physical desire she'd created in him was powerful, demanding fulfillment.

"You're not afraid of getting up close and friendly with some guy you've just met?"

"I teach self-defense classes, mister. If anyone should be afraid, you should." Her quirky grin reassured him she was an adult with all her faculties.

He gave a slow nod, pleased with her response. There was a definite sense of inevitability about what was happening between them—there was no turning back—but he respected her attitude. She was the kind of strong, self-assured woman he was attracted to, but rarely met.

He reached out one finger to trace her jawline. "I've got a hotel room a few streets away. It's an end-of-tour perk for after the party tonight."

"Wonderful . . . but, wouldn't I be keeping you from the party?" She looked closely at him as she asked, and there was a serious, intense look in her eyes then that made him crave more of her.

"Right now I'm more interested in the party we can make on our own." He was totally focused on her, and the party felt a million miles away. In fact, he couldn't have given a toss about what was going on in the hospitality suite, not anymore.

"We can always drop by later," he added, wondering at the same time if that was playing right into her plans to get backstage, but dismissing it just as quickly when her hand closed on his dick.

"In that case, let's go," she whispered, her eyes gleaming with devilment in the moonlight.

Chapter Two

The hotel was a compact, modern building, squeezed down a back street near Leicester Square. Kelly darted out of the elevator and along the corridor, until he snatched her back into his arms. Her heart raced, her blood pounded. He'd had his hands all over her, and now they were chasing after each other, practically bouncing off the walls as they kissed and groped their way toward their destination.

"You're not going to get all rock and roll on me, and trash the joint?" she teased, when they tripped over a tray that someone had left outside a room, sending the empty teacups rattling in their saucers.

"I'm not that kind of roadie," he replied, with a wry smile, "but

I do have music." He tapped his jacket over the inside breast pocket.

"Excellent." She kissed him again, briefly running her hands over his chest before backing away.

"Not so fast," he said as she tried to break free, locking her against the wall between two doorways.

Kelly glanced over his shoulder, catching sight of the room they were looking for. She laughed and nodded her head at the door behind him. "Your hotel room is behind you, mister."

Without looking, he turned around with her captured in his arms, and backed her toward the room, his powerful legs shifting hers.

For a woman as strong and independent as she tried to be, his power and attitude hit her like a force ten. The need for sexual combat and the desire to do battle with him ratcheted up inside her, sending her body into overdrive. She was powerfully aroused, ready to fuck hard.

Holding her up against the door, he rode his body up and down against hers.

"You must have liked it when I did that to you," she breathed. "You keep returning the favor."

"Too right," he answered, the corners of his mouth lifting.

She could feel the hard bones of his hips, the muscles of his thighs and his cock bulging as he moved against her. Her breath dashed out, the direct contact making her dizzy. Her head rolled from side to side; she was flooded with unleashed lust—she had to have action soon. She reached out and gave his jaw a gentle bite. The shape of it was so appealing, she was constantly drawn to touch, kiss, and bite it.

He murmured something unintelligible, pulled the key card from his back pocket, and held it over the slot. He paused. "I want you to know that I don't usually do this."

That tickled her. He might be the big, tough man, the world-traveled roadie, but he seemed to be a bit of an old-fashioned sort too. She reached for the card key, taking it from him and tapping the end of his nose with it. "Don't worry, I'll be gentle with you." She waggled her eyebrows.

"You cheeky madam." His eyes flashed at her, his handsome mouth breaking into a wide grin. He snatched the key card back and swiped it decisively.

The door clicked open, and she turned into the room, laughing, willing him to chase her.

The room was small, functional, and dimly lit by a lamp on the bedside table. A big bottle stood next to the lamp, dressed up in a bow. Someone had sent him champagne. Clayton, she guessed. She got maybe five feet away when he grabbed her from behind, his hands on her hips, thumbs looping over the waistband on her hipsters.

"I thought we agreed you deserve to be punished?"

She wriggled in his hold.

He loosed one hand and smacked her across her right buttock.

She yelped. Even through the leather of her hipsters the smack shot into her, melting her to the spot. Her pulse raced, a heady mixture of rampant lust and the will to challenge him taking hold of her. She broke free and dived at the bed.

She made it onto the surface of the bed and was on her hands and knees scrabbling over it, laughing, when he snatched at one of her ankles. Pulling her knees from under her, he had her flat on the bed. Climbing over her, he captured her between his knees. He pushed his hands around her waist to reach for her zipper.

Realizing his intention was to keep her pinned down while he stripped her, she wriggled and jabbed with her elbows, making the task as difficult as possible. *He's going for the pants.* It sent a thrill through her, but she wasn't going down easily.

"Like it rough do you, Kelly?"

Oh yes, she thought. He'd said that back at the concert too, and somewhere deep inside she knew she wanted that, and wanted it badly. She growled back at him, answering in actions, flashing her eyes as she glanced over her shoulder at him.

He loomed over her, his face in shadow as he wrenched the hipsters down, taking her G-string with them. She clenched her thighs together when she felt her bottom being bared. He bent down and bit her right buttock, marking her skin. The sharp, sudden sensation winded her and she flattened against the bed, her limbs growing momentarily limp. He took advantage of the situation and dragged the pants down the length of her legs.

"You have the most spectacular arse," he commented. "I'm going to enjoy spanking it. I want to see it marked with the imprint of my hand."

She moaned, pushing her face into the bed covers. Her sex was on fire at the thought of his hands on her, forcing her to take it.

The sound of her moan seemed to fuel him, because he moved faster, lifting her torso bodily from the bed and then letting her drop down when he'd untied her top and dropped it on the floor. He moved down to her feet. Lifting one foot, he undid the laces on her Doc Martens, prized off one boot and sock, then the other. Tugging her pants and underwear down and off, he had her naked and facedown on the bed within seconds of them entering the room.

So much for putting up a fight. She chuckled, rising to her knees.

He sat down heavily beside her and snatched her into his arms, hauling her over his thighs.

"No," she cried. Humiliation flashed through her.

"Oh, yes." Planting his legs wide to support her, he draped her over them, with her breasts hanging over one leg, her bottom angled up on the other. He stroked the surface of her right buttock with his large, warm palm, moving in a circular motion, and then clutched the cheek in his hand, before moving away.

Smack. Raw pain seared her bare skin. *He really meant it.* She hadn't been expecting this. A playful spank when he'd given chase, yes, but this was something else.

"Tell me if it's too much. I'll forgive you if you can't take it," he said, chuckling.

She couldn't withhold a whimper. He'd given her an out, a safety zone, but she bit her lip, unwilling to admit defeat so early on.

He moved his attention to the other buttock, ignoring her whimper. He had one hand against her back, holding her in place over his lap. The other was now working her other buttock up for that first smack.

The waiting was unbearable, and then she noticed the shadows moving on the floor, elongated, and yet clearly delineating the movement of her prone body. The light was behind her. *Fuck.* He'd got her on the side of the bed where the lamp stood—he'd be able to see everything from the light thrown onto her splayed bottom.

Her sex squeezed tight in response to that realization, and she felt moisture trickle down her labia, maddening her.

The second spank came, and then he moved his attention back to the first, smacking it several times in quick succession before going back to the second buttock and repeating.

Pain shot through her, but by the third time something else was roaring through her veins, too—a crazed, euphoric feeling. Pleasure was fast becoming bound up with the pain, a strange, growing force taking her over like some sort of drug. Her entire midsection was hot too, painfully hot and aroused, his actions pushing her further into a state of frenzy with every passing second.

His hand moved again, but instead of repeating the pattern, he plunged it in between her thighs, clutching her exposed pussy.

It was so unexpected that she cried out with surprise, her entire body jerking up in response.

"You have the most gorgeous derriere," he said, thrusting his thumb into her hole, while he worked his forefinger against her clit. "And your pussy looks delicious, so wet, you naughty girl."

Her head nearly blew off when he moved his knuckle back and forth over her clit in time with his thumb inside her. Humiliation, pain, and pleasure were strange bedfellows, but Kelly was assailed with all three, and she was enjoying every moment of it. She moaned and thrashed, saliva gathering in her mouth. She could hear the slurp of her wet pussy as he worked into it with his thumb. He'd gotten total control of her. Just as she'd been powerless over his shoulder back at the concert, he had her over his knee and was doing exactly what she had wished for back then—he was taking her, using her, filling her. And it was good.

Her fingernails scraped the carpet, clutching, feeble and power-less as he worked his thumb into her. "Oh that is so good," she blurted.

"You like that, huh?"

"Yes," she said, pushing her bottom back, easing her pussy into a better angle on his hand. She wasn't aware of anything outside of the drive for fulfillment. "Feels so good, I'm on fire." She bucked her hips, when she felt his thumb rubbing against the front wall of her sex. "You're going to make me come."

"Oh, yes, several times, in fact." He moved his hand, riding it in and out of her pussy.

She cried out, her inner muscles clenching on to him, wanting his hand, wanting something else too: that massive hard cock of his. "Fuck me, please," she cried out, her face burning.

He gave a dark chuckle, and worked her even harder. "We have to deal with your punishment first, and every time you answer me back you will get spanked again."

She blinked away her blurring vision. She didn't know what she wanted more of first, even if she could decide. He was in charge right now, and he could use her as he wished.

"Do it then. Hurry," she demanded. She swallowed, resting her fingertips on the floor for balance.

"That's better." He moved the hand he had on her back lower, stroking her tingling buttocks while he still worked her with his other hand. He moved his fingers to the crease at the base her spine and stroked one finger into it. She was already on overload, about to come, when he ran a finger over her anus.

She had to blink and make an extreme effort to concentrate to keep from falling. As he moved that finger into her anus, easing it inside, her body lost focus. She became a clutching, writhing creature, controlled totally by his hands on her.

"Tommy," she gasped, but it was too late to beg him to slow down, too late to try to hang on. Her hips ground against him of their own accord, muscles clutching at the hard intrusion of his thumb as she shuddered into release.

She struggled for breath. For several moments, she lost touch with where she was, then she felt his hand stroking her back again, soothing her, his breath warm on her back, a gentle kiss dropped on her shoulder, his voice murmuring in the background. He had extracted his finger and thumb, and was caressing the sensitive folds of her pussy with tender, inquisitive fingers.

Panting, she grasped his thighs with her hands, making an extreme effort to speak. "Tommy, let me up, please. I am about to pass out."

He rolled her easily in his arms, lifting her against him and rising to his feet. "Too much for you?" The smile on his face was wicked.

Never. Quickly gathering herself, she took a deep breath then exhaled it on a casual laugh. "It was pretty good . . . for openers." *Take that for a challenge, mister.*

He gave a dark laugh, then lowered her and rolled her onto the bed.

Once again she found herself winded. This man was like a force of nature. Struggling to get off the covers, she managed to push herself up, still shaking in the aftermath of her orgasm, and looked over at him.

His jacket was on the floor. He was busy plugging his iPod into the sound system. Hard rock wheeled up around them, filling the room with atmospheric-chugging guitars. The music beat in her blood, rousing her with its powerful rhythm, while she feasted on the sight of him stripping. He kicked off his shoes and pulled his T-shirt over his head. His torso mesmerized her in a split-second. She had felt that strength and power under her hands, but seeing it naked was something else altogether.

His pecs were well-defined, his shoulders huge. As he moved to drop the T-shirt on the floor, his biceps were cast in light, then shadow, emphasizing their shape and strength. She noticed the hard wall of muscle in his stomach, as he snapped at the buckle of his belt and went for his zipper. His six-pack rippled with movement as he shoved his jeans down the strong columns of his thighs.

She rolled onto her side, supporting herself on one elbow as she took in the sight of his black Jockey shorts. They were softly molded to his hips, the erection just about captured inside, like the stout branch of a tree bowing out.

"Great bod," she murmured under her breath, smiling when he paused and glanced her way.

"Don't you get too relaxed, madam." He kicked the jeans off, then snatched them back up and reached into the back pocket for his wallet.

"Oh, I'm not relaxed at all, believe me." She blew him a kiss, nodding at the bulge in his shorts.

Pulling out a packet of condoms, he tore one off and dropped the rest on the bedside table

Kelly rolled closer and snatched the condom packet from his hand. "Allow me to assist."

His hair fell forward as he looked down at her, casting his face in shadow, but she could see the tension in his mouth, his lips tightly closed. He pushed his shorts down, kicking them off. His cock bounced out, seeming to lean toward her with intent. It was long and hard, the head burnished red and damp in the lamplight.

She'd barely recovered from the assault he'd launched on her, but her sex responded, her entire core moving in a reflex action triggered by the need to feel that gorgeous, hard cock inside her. She moved closer, wrapped her hand around its girth, stroking it back and forth. It was hot and rigid, buoying up within her grasp.

"Easy," he urged and she saw his thighs tighten.

With shaking fingers, she tore open the condom packet. Looking at the rubber, it seemed impossibly small. She rolled it over the head of his cock, struggling to ease it on. She rolled it the length of him, using both hands. The hair at the base of his cock was golden, catching the light when he moved.

When the condom was in position, she reached for his balls. He groaned when she felt them, weighing them in her hands. They were already high against the underside of his cock. Her inner flesh trembled at the thought of the release.

He knocked her away with one hand, pushing her back onto the bed. "Lie down, on your back."

Rolling back, her knees automatically drew up toward her chest, her body inviting him in.

He shook his head as he looked down at her. "What a sight." He ducked down, his hands on the base of his cock as he dipped in to take a taste of her, running his tongue into her hole, then lapping at her clit.

Once again he took her by surprise. She flung her arms back over her head; her sensitive sex folds in a frenzied torment. "Oh, you're good, big man."

"I've got to be inside you," he said gruffly, as he moved between her thighs and guided his cock into her.

"Mmm, yes please."

He nudged inside her, the head of his cock stretching her, even though she was open and ready.

"You're so big," she gasped. The sensitized entrance of her sex clenched on to him.

"Watch the mouth. Compliments can undermine a man's stamina." He winked.

She laughed softly; she could see the honesty of his words reflected in his eyes.

"Yeah, good," he whispered, with a quick grin as her legs came around his hips. Their eyes locked as he drove himself slowly into her, inch by inch, filling her up. When the head of his cock nudged up against her cervix, a strangled cry escaped her. Suddenly full, she felt dizzy.

He lifted up on his arms, his hands planted on either side of her chest. He began to move, slowly at first then with more urgency. The music seemed to drive him on, and he pounded into her. The singer had a deep, gravelly voice that touched her inside, as surely as Tommy was doing.

Kelly could only ride it out. Her body was on fire, and although she wanted to fight and equal him, she was too weak with pleasure. He had sensitized her so thoroughly she was like a rag doll on the bed. Lyrics from the stereo reached her. *"Just let it happen,"* the singer encouraged, his voice rising in the chorus. The words skittered over her consciousness, drawing on her. Heat was gathering as high as her rib cage, darts of stimulation racing through her breasts and into her nipples with each thrust of her body across the bed. Her eyes held his, one hand clutching feebly at his shoulder. "I've never been so well and truly fucked," she cried out, her body humming.

He groaned and pulled out. His hand went to the base of his cock, where he applied pressure. "I warned you," he rasped. "Say something like that and it's likely to result in a sudden explosion."

"I'm hoping to be victim of a sudden explosion at some point," she retorted, with a low laugh.

He gave her a quick grin, and then grabbed her hip with his free hand, rolling her over. Before she had a chance to respond, both his hands were on her hips and he'd pulled her into a kneeling position. The movement against the bed made her buttocks twinge, his hands on their raw surface sending an aftershock through her. Before she had time to breathe, his cock was back inside her.

A slower but more powerful track had started up, one with a distinctly strip-joint rhythm to the guitars. The song opened and a powerful flash of guitar music led the singer, his voice delivering a compelling chant. Her hips moved in time, unable to resist the rhythm.

Tommy gave a low laugh and his hands slapped onto her waist, stinging her as he held on to her swaying body.

The sensation shot through her and she stretched her neck, her chin jutting forward and her eyes closing. Her body had never been so thoroughly wired, her dark side so thrilled.

He pushed her thighs together with his knees, locking her on to him, and he was thrusting so vigorously that she felt each movement riding up through her center, into her throat, where it left a burning sensation. Her core melted, clenched. She was coming, again. Her mouth went dry as her sex filled with bolt after bolt of release, a rolling orgasm hitting her suddenly. Her fingers clutched uselessly at the bedcovers, her head hanging down.

"Yes, Kelly," he whispered, and then she felt his hands hold her in against him where he rolled his hips, never breaking the contact, the head of his cock pushing her cervix high.

She was barely recovering when she felt his fingers moving around his cock as he plunged in and out, then one reached higher, smoothing over her anus. She shivered, involuntarily.

He eased his finger inside her anus.

She felt suddenly full in every way, her sex stretched by his mighty cock, her anus open and being massaged by his hard finger, the knuckle nudging her ring, sending hot flares up her spine with each small movement.

His cock stroked faster. He was taking more shallow thrusts, lifting against the spot his finger invaded for friction. She heard him panting, felt his body taut and jerking as if he couldn't keep the rhythm. He was close.

His finger moved, pushing deeper, and pure fire sped up her spine. His cock jerked and lifted, he pulled his finger out, but his climax had brought her back to her peak again, her entire lower body suffused with pleasure as she tripped into a higher plateau, multiple climaxes hitting her.

Moments passed. His hand on her back, stroking her, leveled her off, and she struggled for breath, her body trembling. "Easy girl," he murmured.

It was then that she realized it was a good job he was holding her, because her hands had slipped from under her, her breasts crushed on the bed. His hands anchoring her hips against his was the only thing keeping her from collapsing in a heap.

He pulled his cock free, and she lifted herself onto her hands. His arms went around her waist and he drew her up against him. Kissing her shoulder, he pushed her hair away from her ear and kissed her there too.

"Good . . . for openers?"

Smiling, she reached one hand back and around his head, embracing him. "Good," she conceded.

She had the strangest blue eyes, Tommy noticed. In the lamplight, they were almost opaque. She was looking at him with intense curiosity now, while they took a break. They'd collapsed together, hot and exhausted. He'd gotten up and found a glass, opened the champagne, and selected something more relaxing on the iPod.

After a while, she climbed over him, lying on top of his body and wedging her chin up on one hand, her elbow resting on his shoulder. "Mind if I warm myself on you?"

"Not at all."

Her toes wriggled and she smiled down at him. "My very own heated, personal bed slave."

A soft laugh escaped him. "I'm no slave."

"I could take that as a challenge."

"You take everything as a challenge, I assume?"

She nodded happily, stroking his neck under his ear.

He swore, swatting her hand off. He had a dangerous erogenous zone there that he guarded with his life. She seemed to be drawn to it like a homing pigeon.

"What?"

"Tickles," he said, gruffly.

"I'll have to remember that, purely for torture purposes."

Apparently her playful streak never let up.

He moved his hands to her buttocks, holding her. She flinched and gave out the deepest, most pleasured sigh. He massaged her gently there, where he'd marked her, claiming her gorgeous arse. He was getting hard again. It wouldn't be long until he was ready to have her all over again.

But, he reminded himself, there was the small matter of discussing whatever it was that she'd seen in Clayton's dressing room. He reached for the glass of champagne and lifted it to her lips. She sipped slowly, never breaking eye contact. Her eyes twinkled. She had a wild nature, and a confrontational attitude that hooked his curiosity.

"It seems a crime to drink such good champagne from a glass made for a toothbrush," she commented, her tongue darting out to lick a spill from her lips.

He set the glass down and kissed the place she had licked, tasting the champagne on her skin.

"Do you always get champagne after a gig?"

He shook his head. "It's been Clayton's biggest tour to date. I traveled all over Europe with him. The room and the champagne are like a bonus." The question brought Clayton back to mind again, the party, and the fact that this little rogue groupie was probably just about to pump him for information.

"You were behind the clothes rail, weren't you?" He touched the tip of her nose. "When I saw you run out of there, I figured it was the only place you could have been. Was I right?"

She nodded. "You were looking straight at me." Her eyes twinkled. "I thought you were going to come over and haul me out."

"That might have been fun."

"You had your fun."

And he wanted more. At the back of his mind, though, a sense of duty and loyalty reminded him that he should be asking her what she'd seen. "How did you know that Clayton and Jay were . . . together?"

She lifted her chin as she gave a soft, breathy laugh. "Because they got rather intimate while I was in there."

"Right, I see." That was bad news. He didn't see anything mercenary in her expression, though. "Are you going to use the information in any way?"

She stared at him a moment, as if his comment hadn't quite sunk in, and then she pulled back, looking a bit horror-struck. "No way. Everyone is entitled to their privacy." She gave a slight frown, looking sheepish. "I know, I intruded on their privacy, but really I didn't know I was intruding on anything of that nature did I?"

Tommy pushed away the thought that she might have been willing to step into Jay's shoes and get intimate with Clayton herself, had Jay not already been in there doing the job. "Clayton is a friend, as well as an employer. I'm concerned that this information will get out."

She shook her head. "I know you don't know me and you don't know if you can trust me, but believe me, you can. That's not my thing at all." She locked eyes with him as she ran her fingers into his hair.

He tried to get the measure of her. His gut instinct said to trust her. But, beyond driving the message home, there was little else he could do, in reality.

"You're a good pal."

"Yes, but I never let a client down. It's my first duty to ensure he's able to do his thing without too much personal hassle."

"Never let a client down, hmm?" She reached for his hips, stroking him.

"That's me." His dick was stirring. "The party will be in full swing. Would you like to go?" She was interested in more sex, he could tell, but he wanted to know what her answer would be.

"And spoil this moment? No way." She reached forward and gave his jawline a gentle bite; it was the oddest little quirk, as if she were marking her territory. "If you need to go," she said, drawing back, looking apologetic, "don't worry, I understand."

"No, I'm happy here." He tried not to be too pleased about the fact that she didn't want to go to the party. It didn't mean anything. "You don't have to get home?"

"No, I'm a big girl, and I can take care of myself."

"I can see that." He laughed softly, enjoying the weight of her body on his, even more since she had chosen him over the party.

She lifted one shoulder in a shrug. "Like I said, life is short." She got that intense serious expression on her face again. It was almost wistful. He felt her pulling back, and it made him curious.

"That's a very hedonistic attitude you've got there."

She gave a dismissive nod, which surprised him.

"Yes, and when something good comes by, you know, you just have to go with the flow . . . enjoy the moment for what it's worth."

"The moment?" He could feel her backing away all the time,

and yet at the very same time her fingers began to clutch at him, her eyes growing dark as she looked at his arms, stroking the muscles there.

"The night." She rose up and moved down to stroke his torso with her hands.

It's a one-night stand. He'd been getting hard anyway, but reference to the temporal situation had his dick up and needy for more, before it was gone. Before she was gone.

"Oh that's good," she said, when she felt his erection against her bottom. Her legs splayed to either side of him.

She put out her hand and he passed her the condom.

She rolled it on quickly, eager, and mounted him, easing him inside and slowly lowering down onto him, her eyes closing in appreciation.

He grabbed her wrists, holding them down, pinning her to the bed. "Do your best to move. I want to see you struggle."

"Are you challenging me?"

"Yes, because you love it."

"How do you know that already?"

"I'm observant."

At first she struggled in his grip, and that was good. His dick was totally enclosed by her warm, damp cunt, each move she made causing minute friction so intense that he felt his whole body driving up into her.

Then she fell still. She didn't move, but, oh, she did! Her inner muscles took over, gripping his rigid dick with regular contractions, her hips rocking back and forth imperceptibly. She gave him a dark stare, her expression filled with challenge. "Can't stop me doing that, can you?"

He gritted his teeth when he felt those deep, rhythmic contractions; he was about to come. He gripped her wrists tighter still, pulling her body down hard and still onto the spurting head of his dick. She cried out in pleasure, her body rippling as she matched him, her cunt seizing, getting tighter still as she came, the inside of her thighs flooding wet.

He pulled her down to his chest, stroking her hair as they surfaced. "You're a crazy lady, Kelly."

"Yeah," she breathed, onto his chest, "and you like that."

She wasn't wrong there.

Chapter Three

Tommy squinted into the light that poured through the open curtains. It took him a few moments to work out where he was, then the soft, warm weight of a woman against his shoulder and chest reminded him. He smiled and glanced down at her. Her breathing was deep and even, her hair a mess on his upper arm.

What a night.

He hadn't even noticed the curtains in the room were open when they got there. They had been far too interested in each other. A chuckle rumbled through his chest and he quelled it in case it woke her, but it didn't seem to disturb her. She was sleeping deeply and he rolled her onto the other pillow.

She drew her knees up toward her chest as she settled into position. The curve of her back was quite beautiful. It brought about a sense of yearning in him, to wake with a woman every morning.

Not this one.

No, she'd made that quite clear. But a woman like her. He hadn't thought about it in a while. He didn't have time for much social life, what with the security work on top of developing the business he part owned with his sister and brother-in-law. Kelly made him think about it again, though.

Why? *Because she is a wild woman out of control.* He laughed at himself. Yes, that was his fantasy type. Not exactly the type of woman you can plan a secure future with. And yet she looked tranquil, sleeping, her body soft and gentle, unlike the wild clamoring thing of the night before. He smiled, remembering. Her bottom looked so good, no longer pink from his spanking. She'd liked that, a lot, though. The feeling of his hands on her; she'd said it brought her pleasure and pain, heating her up for his dick. He loved the way she told him exactly what it had done to her. He was getting hard at the memory of it.

It made him feel possessive and he reached out and stroked her buttock gently with one hand, remembering how it had felt when she'd wrapped her legs around his hips in the corridor backstage. Just holding her bottom in his hands, while she'd ground her crotch against him, had sent him crazy. There had been no turning back from that point on. That's all she had wanted though, one night. Regretfully, he faced the fact.

She murmured in her sleep and clutched at the covers. He moved away, wondering if she was cold. Reaching down to the end of the bed, he pulled the comforter over her. She snuggled into the pillow and her breathing fell into a regular pattern again.

He stood and stretched, glancing out the window. It looked out onto an alleyway. He couldn't get over the fact that they hadn't even noticed the curtains were open. The idea made him feel good. It had been a hot night, raunchy as hell. Shame she only wanted the one night.

What about the fact that you said you'd never sleep with a groupie?

There it was. His conscience had woken up and was bugging him with the question he'd managed to push aside for the whole of the night before. It wasn't so easy to ignore it now, in the morning light.

She'd been after Clayton, the star. She was probably gutted Clayton was gay, and he'd been a convenient lay—second choice— since she couldn't get her hands on the star himself. It had been a mistake. It happened a lot in the business, many of the backstage crew took one-nighters with groupies wherever they could, but not him.

Until now?

He'd sworn he would never go for that. But she'd seemed so interested in him; turned on from the moment he captured her. She'd loved the sex games; playing up to his punishment performance like it was the best sex she'd ever had.

You broke your vow, his conscience nagged on.

He picked up his phone from the bedside table to check the time and noticed that he'd received a text message in the early hours.

U r an uncle! Queen Elizabeth's hospital. Carol & baby doing fine. Jim.

Tommy stared at the screen in surprise. His little sister had delivered six weeks early. An unexpected bolt of pride hit him. Reaching for his abandoned jeans, he pulled them on quickly, hopping about on one foot, wondering if it was a girl or a boy. A boy, he hoped—he liked the idea of having a nephew. His clothes and shoes were scattered everywhere. He strode about, collecting them, and wondered whether he should wake Kelly.

When he was dressed, he returned to the bedside. It seemed a shame to wake her, especially for what was bound to be an awkward post-one-night-stand good-bye. Given what she had said the night before, she would probably prefer that he didn't. He unplugged his iPod, pushed it into his hip pocket, and then glanced about. The room had been paid for in advance. There was a hostess tray, so, whenever she woke, she could have coffee, shower and leave in her own time. He'd have liked to see her again, but she wouldn't want that. He reached for his leather jacket.

Admit it, his conscience said, *it was a mistake—you broke your vow. She wanted sex. She'll only give you the cold shoulder. It was good but it's over.*

Running his fingers through his hair, he nodded, but he still felt torn. She was a lot of fun, a truly wild woman. He stepped closer and smoothed her hair back from her forehead. She gave a little snore, and he smiled. Turning away, he pulled his jacket on and quietly left the room.

*H*e was gone. Kelly wasn't sure why she felt such a big sense of loss, but she did. She hadn't wanted any more than what they had shared. She never did. *I don't need a man.* Her independence was something she wore like a badge of courage, like a shield. There's no way she wanted to become dependent on another person. Her mother had been destroyed by the breakup of her marriage, and since her father left them when she was five years old, Kelly had never wanted anything from men other than a bit of fun. It was sensible. She called it self-protection.

But even as she sat up in the bed mulling it over, her eyes went to the dent in the sheet where he'd lain, the crease in the pillow where he'd folded it over and tucked it under to get closer to her as they had fallen asleep—and she wished he were there.

Suddenly annoyed, she threw back the sheets and leaped off the bed. "Would have been nice just to say good-bye," she muttered, snatching her clothes up from the floor. Among them, she found the abandoned champagne cork. Picking it up, she hurled it at the bathroom door. As she did, the door swung open and she saw a reflection of herself in the mirror from the bathroom. She looked a mess, with her top hastily pulled on and her leather pants hanging from her hand. *His fault.*

Sometimes she hated looking in the mirror because she saw her mother, heartbroken. They shared the same intensity and the same eyes. Kelly had decided when she was six years old that she never wanted to be heartbroken like that. She'd steeled herself against it.

"Men," she said to herself, vehemently, and began to pull her pants on. Okay, so she had told him she only wanted the night, but they could have pretended to trade phone numbers. That's what she usually did if she met a bloke she liked, giving him her number and then ignoring her phone, screening each and every call. He could have at least pretended to exchange numbers, at least tried to be polite. She might have even answered the phone for this one.

She was smarting badly. She paced up and down, trying to work off some of her indignation. Letting it go would be the best thing to do, she knew that, but something was niggling at her. She hadn't wanted him to be gone.

You don't need a man, she reminded herself. Nothing to lose, best way to be.

When she was fully dressed, she pushed her hair back and stormed out of the room with her head held high.

Tommy was observing his little sister holding the new baby, while Jim stood by looking foolishly happy with his new perma-grin, when he realized just how stupid he'd been. So what if Kelly had indicated it was only a one-night stand? He should have made a bigger effort to show he would have been interested in more.

Seeing his sister and Jim so infinitely happy had led him to question himself. Jim and Carol hadn't exactly had an easy beginning, logic pointed out, why should anyone else? They'd run into each other at a holiday resort in Spain, literally. It had been Carol's last night there, and Jim had just arrived. They stumbled into each other in a nightclub. He'd spilled his drink on her but she forgave him. He bought her another. They spent barely an hour together. The next day Carol flew out, and they hadn't even exchanged numbers. His tenacious little sister hadn't let that stop her. She tracked Jim down by telling the story on a London radio station, and Jim had heard her and called.

"Carol, I've got something I have to do, and I'm afraid I'm going to have to leave."

His sister nodded, and Jim reached over and put out his hand.

"Thanks for coming so quickly," his brother-in-law said. "Uncle Tommy." He grinned.

Tommy took his hand, shaking it and saluting. "No worries. I'll come back later on this evening." He reached over to kiss Carol on the forehead. "Sorry, sis. It's just something urgent I need to attend to, I'll explain later."

"You wanted a nephew," she accused gently, smiling.

"No, I wanted a precocious little madam like my little sis." He'd always called Carol "madam," it was a term of endearment. But he'd called Kelly that too, he remembered, and realized that it had felt right, that's why. *Go back to the hotel, bozo.*

He stroked the little one's cheek with the back of his finger, feeling somehow clumsy and too big, but needing to communicate with this new member of their family. "She's beautiful."

Carol squeezed his hand, nodding.

Seconds later he jogged out of the hospital and onto the street, waving for a taxi as he did so. "Leicester Square," he shouted as he jumped into the cab.

What the hell was I thinking? He'd had the best night, with a stunning, exciting woman, and he'd just left. He shoved his head in his hands, glancing out of the window every now and then to check on the journey's progress.

When the taxi reached the hotel, he pushed the cash at the driver and darted into reception. He didn't stop to ask; he went straight to the stairs, jogging up to the second floor. His heart sank when he got to the room. The door was open, the laundry cart outside indicating that the room was being made over for the next guests. He stood in the doorway, looking at the empty bed, the sheets still scattered from where she'd pushed them back when she got out of bed. In the bathroom, he could see the maid was busy mopping.

"Excuse me, did you see the woman leave?"

The maid jumped, her expression shocked, and put her hand on her chest. "Bloody hell, mate. My old ticker's not made for this."

"Sorry, I didn't mean to startle you." He nodded back at the bed. "Did you see the lady leave?"

"Sorry, can't help you, room was empty when I got this far, didn't see anyone."

He nodded, thanking her. Outside in the corridor, he saw two of Clayton's entourage emerging from a room farther down the hallway. The woman waved and said something about the night before. He returned the wave but turned away quickly. He was far too annoyed with himself to exchange pleasantries.

Running a hand through his hair he worked back through what had happened the night before, everything that had been said. All he knew was that her name was Kelly. That was it. He cursed himself for the way he'd handled it. The situation had to be blamed for making him lose any sense of reality, though. What happened between them had been crazy. He hadn't been able to think straight, only act on instinct, and now he had no clue where or who the hell she was.

"Nice going, bozo," he muttered, as he descended the stairs.

And then," Helen paused to grin, "when he came out for the final encore, he'd taken the shirt off." She fanned herself with one hand, holding out her phone for Jojo in the other. A blurred picture of Clayton Warren was captured on the screen.

Kelly looked on and smiled wryly to herself.

"Details, details." Jojo's eyes gleamed as she stared at the blur and waited for Helen to describe Clayton's stage appearance just one more time.

Helen obliged the request with pleasure, cataloguing Clayton's physique in detail.

Kelly poured them another glass of wine, trying to avoid staring at the pins poking out of Jojo's leg. She'd just about die, if she had to sit around looking at that on the end of her leg. Not only was she addicted to exercise; she couldn't actually sit still for any length of time. Easily bored, she quickly turned obnoxious when kept indoors. She was a monster when she had a head cold, let alone a full-blown injury. Jojo was being incredibly patient, and they'd been doing their best to keep her entertained.

"Why don't you ask Kelly," Helen said. "She got to see him up close and personal, backstage."

Kelly started when Helen's comment reached her. She glanced up from her wineglass, her mind suddenly filled with the image of Clayton "up close and personal, backstage." She laughed to herself. "Oh, Helen is so much better at describing him than I am."

Jojo nodded. "Thanks for trying to get me the autograph, you're a star."

"She was a woman on a mission," Helen said. "If anyone could have done it, Kelly could."

Kelly smiled. "But I failed." She said it with a sigh and a depth of emotion that was based more on her interaction with Tommy than with Clayton.

"Was he as gorgeous up close?" Jojo's eyes were sparkling. She was practically in heat, just thinking about Clayton.

Oh, the irony, thought Kelly. "He was very attractive, but I'm no good at this. He's not my type," she offered, as an excuse. *He's not your type either*, she mused. She wasn't tempted to share the information, though. What was the point of shattering Jojo's dream? Besides, it was a secret, and, like she had told Tommy, she wasn't the sort of woman to break the code on real, deep, and meaningful secrets.

"Kelly doesn't like metrosexuals," Helen commented.

Jojo frowned. "What the hell is a 'metrosexual'?"

"You know, a bloke that looks after his appearance, reads magazines, does skin care, that sort of thing. He might be a rock god but Clayton Warren looks after himself. I could tell."

Jojo looked relieved. "Oh, right." She glanced at Kelly, smiling. "Yes, you do like them a bit more rugged than that, don't you? So, tell us, was this hunky security man rugged enough for you?" She waggled her eyebrows, shifting in her chair to get more comfy for the story.

He hadn't been far from her mind anyway, but he was back in full detail now. "Oh yes, he was rugged all right."

"She's been moping around all day," Helen said. "I think she should go after him. I've never seen her like this, have you?"

"She's definitely got a pout on," Jojo agreed, swigging her wine.

"Stop talking about me as if I'm not here."

"You might as well not be," Helen commented. "You're pretty fixed on this bloke, aren't you?"

"No," she responded, indignant.

Helen snorted.

"Okay, I guess I've been a bit preoccupied since last night."

"Last night . . . that would be when you rolled in at god-knows-what-time, young lady?" Helen folded her arms across her chest, peering across at Kelly and doing a fair impression of a disapproving mother figure.

Despite her mood, Kelly managed to smile. "This morning."

"Dare I ask if you had a good time?" Jojo said, with curiosity.

Kelly sighed. "It was the best sex I ever had."

Jojo shifted awkwardly in her chair, focusing her attention on Kelly. "Go, girl! So, did you get his number?"

"It wasn't like that." *Nothing to lose*, she reminded herself.

"Oh, I see," Helen said, looking smug. "You've done one of your one-night-stand flits on this poor man and now you're regretting it. Admit it."

"Not quite, but kind off." Pride stopped Kelly from pointing out that he had been the one to do the flit, but they had a point. She *was* regretting it.

Jojo watched on with an innocent expression. It was her specialty. "So what's stopping you? If anyone can hunt the man down, you can." She burst out laughing and Helen joined her, reaching over to chink her glass.

Kelly took another sip of her wine as the suggestion began to ricochet in her mind, setting off all sorts of mad ideas. She got to her feet, walking up and down the length of the sitting room. Why the hell not? She could hunt him down. Hell, she'd use him the way he'd used her. *Sexually*. Her body burned with anticipation at the very thought of it. She wanted another night with Tommy and she was going to go after it.

"Ooh, I sense trouble." Jojo faked a scared expression as she watched Kelly pacing up and down.

"I think you've set her off," Helen said.

"Yes, you have." Kelly grinned. "Ladies, if you'll excuse me, I have some research to do."

Jojo saluted her. "Go, soldier. Hunt your target down and hunt him well."

Kelly returned the salute and then darted off to her bedroom, unfazed about the laughter following in her wake.

Inside her room, she flicked her computer on. There was only one way to track Tommy down, and that was through Clayton Warren himself. Her mind whirred over as she considered her options. She'd have to play the groupie all over again, but this time she had to do it more cleverly. She needed to find out Tommy's name and get to him.

She scoured the message boards on Clayton's fan forum. It didn't take long for her to discover that in the wake of his tour, he was spending a few days in the recording studio, before taking a month's vacation. It didn't say which studio, but some quick detective work on the sleeve of his latest CD gave her a name, the Celtic. He may not be using the same venue, but judging from the thank-you messages, he liked the place. It was a good starting point, and she was on an early shift the next morning, so she could stake it out in the afternoon. She could also ring his agent, try for an interview. Ideas were coming fast and furious now.

That night she couldn't sleep, inspired now that she had decided to track him down. "If you thought I was a crazy lady last night, Tommy, just wait till I get ahold of you again."

Smiling into the darkness she rolled across her bed, restless. Her hands roved over her body, sensation flashing beneath her skin as she remembered how hot it had been. She tweaked her nipples, pulling on them as they grew harder. One hand went lower, and she stroked her pussy, squeezing it with her hand, promising herself a night of total pleasure. She would use him; take his glorious body for her own pleasure.

As she squeezed and stroked her labia she pictured his body, his strong muscles trapped, his body bound for her pleasure. One finger tapped her clit, the simple movement setting bolts of stimulation free in her groin. His cock had given her so much intense pleasure, orgasm after orgasm. She wanted to play with it, make it hers again. Her hand grappled for the bedside drawer. Opening it, she pulled out her vibrator. Moonlight glinted off the silver rocket in the darkness. Flicking it on, she ran it over her clit and then lower, into her damp slit.

"Tommy," she whispered. "I want you, and I'm going to have you."

She rode the vibrator in and out, her free hand clutching at her breasts, moving from one to the other, massaging them. They were full with need, her nipples so taut they hurt.

"I'm going to punish you, Tommy, punish you for leaving me." She whispered the words into the darkness. They had crept up suddenly from somewhere deep inside her and, even as she said them, her heart raced up a notch. Yes, he had punished her. Now it was his turn to take it.

Her climax built on the horizon. She moved the vibrator faster, pulling it out to send a rabid hum through her clit with the shaft against it, before shoving it deep inside again.

Raw pleasure and determination to overcome him flew around her veins. When she came, she sat up, wedging the vibrator inside her, a guttural moan filling the room as she ground hard on it, her imagination flying with images of Tommy at her beck and call.

ChapterFour

The Celtic studio was a single doorway wedged in between an alternative clothes shop and an antiquarian bookstore. Glancing up, Kelly guessed the studio itself was upstairs. Sure enough, the windows above the shops on either side were all blacked out and had the studio logo on them. Pulling a map out of her backpack, she adopted a confused expression and walked through the door.

Inside, a narrow hallway led to a small reception area where a figure sat behind a shiny black desk. Plush carpeting silenced her footsteps. The door had closed behind her, blocking out the busy street noise. The place was swish, and soundproofed. The walls were lined with framed vinyl records. Kelly looked at them with curiosity as she passed. The receptionist, a lean punk with a shock of red hair, was dressed in shiny black and would have merged into her black desk, had it not been for the pale skin and the red hair.

"Hi," Kelly said. "I wonder if you could help me. I'm trying to find the quickest route to the nearest underground station, and I'm a bit lost."

The receptionist nodded, barely taking her eyes off her monitor. "Go back out the door, first left, second right. You'll see it straight-away."

"I just realized; this is a recording studio." Kelly smiled, glancing around at the vinyl discs in the frames. "Anyone famous recording today?"

The punk paused on her task, giving Kelly her full attention and delivering a look that said "Don't try that one on me." People had obviously attempted it before. "That information is confidential." She gave a false smile, and returned to her task.

"Yes, of course it is. Thanks for the directions." She took one last, quick look around but couldn't see anything other than a couple of closed doorways that presumably led to the studios upstairs, or the cellar area.

She was about to leave when one of the doors swung open and a woman emerged carrying a bunch of empty coffee cups. She was dressed in black too, but had more of a Goth look about her, with black-and-red-striped hair and kohl-lined eyes. Apparently, you had to look like a music subgenre to work in the biz. Kelly smiled to herself. She was getting a lot of insight into the music world over these past few days, one way or the other.

As the door swung closed behind the Goth, she caught the sound of guitar music. Someone was definitely recording, and it sounded rocky. Hopefully, it was Clayton.

Back in the street she glanced at her watch, pulled an energy drink out of her backpack, and then took up a watching position a few doors away, preparing to wait it out until the elusive recording artist emerged. If it was Clayton, she'd make her move.

The afternoon dragged. She was beginning to think she was on a fool's errand. It was getting toward six in the evening when a figure finally emerged from the Celtic. She gathered herself, pushing her sunglasses up her nose, getting ready to make an approach. Craning her neck, she watched as the man pulled up the collar on his jacket and put on a pair of wraparound shades, glancing around.

It was Clayton. Jay stepped out of the building behind him, hand raised to hail a taxi.

The *Mission Impossible* theme struck up in her head. Cautiously, she began to close in, hope and determination fueling her. Then she saw two teenage girls appear out of nowhere. They approached the two men and seemed to be asking Clayton for his autograph.

Kelly was amazed; she hadn't seen them waiting. They'd been even more surreptitious than she had. No wonder Clayton was wary of groupies. And yet he seemed to be quite friendly and chatted with them while Jay went to the edge of the street and waved down a taxicab. Presumably signing autographs in a public place was acceptable. It was more about privacy than anything else, and she should have realized that right at the beginning. She smiled wryly to herself, sheepishly aware of the error she had made by intruding into his private space.

A momentary doubt hit her; she was going to do just that, all over again. How would he take it? Not well, she knew that, but she thought about Tommy. She wanted to know. This was the only way. A trademark London black cab pulled up beside the two men, and she broke into a jog. If they left now, her wait would have been futile. "It's now or never."

She made it to the door just as Jay disappeared inside, with Clayton already ensconced in the cab. The driver was signaling, readying to pull out into the traffic. She didn't have a choice. She snatched the door from Jay's hand and leaped in behind him.

"Wait up," she said to the driver.

The cab driver paused, watching them in his mirror.

"Hey, this cab is taken." Clayton looked panicked, glancing at Jay for support.

"Out!" Jay pointed at the door of the cab.

Flipping down a seat facing the two of them, she held up her hands. "Okay, I know this looks really bad. I'm just asking you to hear me out." She had to raise her voice over the hum of the engine revving.

"Hear you out?" Jay frowned.

"Wait a minute, you're the groupie from the last night of the tour." Clayton looked even more panicked. "Jay, get rid of her."

"I'm not here to bother you, seriously, please believe me. I'm not a groupie, never was. I was trying to get an autograph for a friend who couldn't make it. I realize I went about it the wrong way and I'm sorry about that. I'm just trying to get in touch with Tommy again. I'd like to um . . . hire him, if I knew how." She attempted to show she was serious. "Please hear me out."

Jay observed her, thoughtful. "We don't have time for this, we've got to be somewhere."

"Please . . . I really want to get in touch with Tommy. That's all it's about." She pursed her lips, giving them her most hopeful expression.

Jay looked at Clayton, one hand on his shoulder, reassuring him. "No harm in hearing what she's got to say."

Clayton didn't look convinced and sank back in his seat, gazing out the window to make a point.

"Thanks, it won't take long and I'll be gone."

"You'll have to tell us on the way," Jay said.

She nodded vigorously.

"Drive on, Piccadilly," Jay called through to the taxi driver, and then looked back at her. "Any trouble from you, and you're out on the street, understood?"

The driver slid shut the glass panel that separated them, and the cab lurched out into the traffic.

Kelly smiled. "Thanks. I really appreciate it. I decided to get in touch with Tommy, but I had no contact number. I don't even know his last name."

The cab was warm, and she could smell that expensive cologne from backstage. Was it Jay's, or Clayton's? Maybe they both wore it. She noticed how Jay had his hand barely touching Clayton, as if his arm was just nonchalantly along the back of the seat, but he was secretly reassuring him. It had to be hard, hiding a secret like that, when all they wanted was to be together. They were living a lie.

"My only option was to come to you, to ask you."

"Pushy sort, aren't you?" Clayton said, clearly rattled by her presence in the cab.

"Yes, I am, I admit that. But you don't get anywhere in life otherwise . . . and it's not like I'm asking for a lot."

Clayton's shoulders were squared, his eyes bright. "I don't owe you anything at all. Most fans are reasonable, but people like you don't respect the fact that I need some space to myself. You seem to think you own a bit of me. You were creeping around backstage on Saturday, now you're in my fuckin' cab. I could call the police."

He wasn't listening to a word she said. Annoyance ratcheted up inside her. She counted to three while reminding herself of his point of view on the situation. His remarks were justified, and she tried to keep her head. "I agree, and you have a point. I shouldn't have been there, but I haven't told anyone I saw you two together."

As soon as the words were out, she knew it was the wrong thing to say, especially right then. Damn.

Jay's head sank back onto the seat, his eyes closing as he shook his head from side to side.

Clayton tensed visibly. He stared at her, his eyes flickering as he took in the implication, his lips tight. "Are you trying to blackmail me?"

Her heart sank, her body tensing. She put up her hand to calm him down. "I'm not trying to blackmail you. I was merely trying to make a point. I shouldn't have intruded on your space on Saturday. I'm sorry, and I'm not here to cause harm. I said that I haven't told anyone that I saw you two together to show you I have no bad intentions. Do you understand?"

Jay lifted his head, his eyes narrowed as he considered her statement.

She directed her words to him. "I could have gone to the press, but I'm not that sort of person. I'm asking you a favor, not trying to blackmail you. All I want is Tommy's contact details. That's it."

Clayton eased back in his seat, still edgy and nervous, but somewhat reassured. "How do I know I can trust you to stay silent about . . . us?" Even saying it was hard for him.

"I respect that you've got a private life, and it is private." She paused for a moment to let her point sink in. "Although, I have to say . . . life would be a lot easier on you if you came out."

Jay smiled at her comment and immediately covered his mouth with his hand, as if he didn't want Clayton to see.

Clayton seemed to develop a nervous twitch at that point, but was apparently unable to come up with a response.

"Clayton has his reasons," Jay explained. "His PR person has advised against it, reckons it might injure the career."

Kelly shook her head. "Sounds as if you should get a new PR person."

"Maybe," Clayton said, grudgingly.

The atmosphere was relaxing, thankfully.

Kelly shook her head. "People come out all the time in the media. In fact, it's likely to get you more attention, not necessarily ruin your career. You know that old saying about there being no such thing as bad publicity."

She had his full attention now. In fact, he was riveted. "Your PR person is showing their prejudice, if you ask me. There will be broken hearts," she smiled, "but it's human interest more than scandal, nowadays. Especially if it's handled right."

Jay's eyes were gleaming. He obviously wanted their relationship out in the open, but was leaving it up to Clayton.

She had their attention, and she was on a roll. "I was reading just the other day that there are a bunch of gay Premier League football players, and they are going to come out together, later this year. The public's gagging for news like this. The press has started to anticipate, rather than denigrate."

Clayton had flopped back on his seat and looked suddenly exhausted. "I don't know if we're ready to face it."

"It would be better coming from you," she added, cautiously. "The next person who inadvertently sees you two together might not be as respectful as me."

"You're not wrong there," Jay said.

Clayton glanced at him, clearly disturbed by that notion.

"Anyway," Kelly continued, trying to guide the conversation back onto steady ground. "I promised Tommy I wouldn't ever tell anyone, not even my mad-for-you housemates. They'd be heartbroken, but they'd learn to live with it, and they'd still buy your music. They love that above all, so even if they think their chances with you are dashed, they'd be there at the next gig, and the one after."

Jay was really struggling to control his smile. "You really like Tommy," he said with a wistful look. "You've gone to a lot of trouble to get in touch with him."

She pursed her lips, unable to deny it, but unwilling to agree. Her motivation was to get one more night of pleasure, and payback. She couldn't let herself forget that. "Let's just say we have unfinished business."

"His name is Tommy Sampson," Clayton said, surprising her and capturing her attention. "He works for me through an agent. We can give you the contact details of the agent, that's your best bet."

"Cheers, that would be great."

Jay reached inside his jacket pocket and pulled out a notepad. He scribbled on it, tore the page out, and handed it over to her

"Thanks, oh, one more thing." She reached into her backpack and pulled out the CD she had brought with her. "Could you please sign this for my friend, Jojo? I came to the gig on her ticket, she was having her leg pinned back together at the time. She broke it skiing."

Jay smiled. "You really were after an autograph?"

Clayton looked from one of them to the other, his expression growing sheepish. He reached out and took the CD. "Sorry," he said. "This business does strange things to your head." He took Jay's pen. "For Jojo, yes?"

Kelly nodded. "It's okay, I understand. You have to be careful. I went about it the wrong way, but it was a spur-of-the-moment thing."

He handed back the signed CD.

Jay watched with a half smile. "What are you planning to do about Tommy? I'm curious. I noticed he never made it to the party that night" He lifted one eyebrow.

"That's true," Clayton commented, laughing softly and looking at her speculatively.

It was good to see him in better humor. For a while there he'd looked like he had the weight of the world on his shoulders. "We had a lot of fun together." She shrugged. "Life is short, so I thought I'd go for a repeat performance." She smiled.

Jay chuckled. "I like your style. In fact, I'll help you get in touch with him, if you like."

"I wanted it to be a surprise," she said, remembering the tentative plan she had put together.

"We can work with that, it will go more smoothly if I give you an intro to his agent. Call it an apology for throwing you out."

She didn't need an apology; throwing her out had been the best thing that had ever happened to her. Something she'd said had touched them, though, she could see that. She put out her hand. "Okay," she agreed.

He shook it.

The cab had drawn to a halt. The driver slid open the glass panel and was waiting for payment.

"I was going to grab a beer while Clayton does an interview. Why don't you join me, and we'll figure something out."

She beamed. "It's a deal."

Tommy glanced through the shop and out of the window at the busy street outside. He was working in a public place, but he was getting a hard-on just thinking about Kelly. He had tried to empty his mind, staring out of the window to focus himself on anything other than filthy thoughts of what he'd like to do to her.

Cars flashed by, interspersed with double-decker red buses. The street was full, the lunchtime rush in full flow. Inside, soft ambient music made the shop feel more tranquil, and it was that that kept making his mind wander. Had to be. He gave in, letting her image drop back into his mind as he watched over the shop.

Being there was giving him a chance to think everything through—rationally. By the middle of the week curiosity and regret had been slowly driving him insane, and he'd decided the only option was to try to track her down, impossible though that might be.

"How's it going?"

The voice pulled him back to the moment and Tommy took the selection of goods that the man, a regular customer, passed over to him: a hard drive, two cables, and a CD stack. "Good, thanks. Carol and the baby are fine and Jim couldn't be happier. Parenthood suits him."

He flicked the mouse on the computer with one hand and put the purchases through the till with the other. He'd been doing Internet searches for women called Kelly all day, while he ran the South London computer parts and repair shop he part owned with Carol and Jim.

He chatted with the customer awhile and after the man had gone, he checked the email account for mail orders, before returning to his hunt through the references to Kellys in London. It was a bit like looking for a needle in a haystack, but he was compelled to try. He hadn't been able to get her out of his head since the moment he'd left her in the hotel room. His conscience kept pricking him, reminding him she was a groupie who hadn't even been interested in him, but he couldn't let it go.

His phone vibrated in his pocket. He glanced at the two customers browsing in the shop. Neither of them seemed to need assistance so he answered the call.

It was Daniel, his agent for security work.

"Hey Dan, how's it going?"

"Good, good. I've got a short contract you might be interested in. Are you up for it?"

"Sure, a short contract would be good, but I'm watching over the shop for my brother-in-law through the rest of this week."

"Should be doable, it's a weekend job," Dan replied.

"In that case, yes. Who is it for? Someone I know?"

."Don't think so, it's an American actress who's flying in for a publicity event. She's got some special requests, a bit unusual, but it was Jay Leonard, Clayton's buddy, that sent her in your direction. She's a pal of his."

Tommy frowned. "What do you mean, special requests?"

"Just stuff I haven't seen before." He laughed dryly into the phone. "Believe me, I've seen some pretty weird requests from clients. It's a top-rate fee, though."

"Go on."

"Basically it looks like she wants the security to be alongside for the entire twenty-four-hour shift. She must have some issues. You will be provided with accommodation at the hotel where she's staying. Looks like she wants a man nearby."

Tommy paused before replying. He had hoped to spend that time tracking Kelly down, but he couldn't afford to turn down a lucrative weekend contract. The extra funds would help Carol and Jim out. He wanted to get some part-time help in the shop, give Jim more time with the baby before coming back to work. "I suppose it makes sense."

"I've got another client to deal with right now, but why don't you come over when you shut up shop this evening, and we'll go over the details then?"

He agreed, put the phone down, and told himself again the cash would help, trying to shrug off the odd feeling he had about the job.

Chapter Five

Tommy was still feeling that there was something odd about the job on Saturday afternoon, when he stepped out of the elevator and glanced up and down the carpeted corridor of the hotel.

It was a cushy place, with solid wood doors and dark walls—a top-class, expensive hotel. He was more familiar with hurrying stars out of back doors and into speeding cars to avoid the press than this sort of number. He'd never had a job quite like it and, while he wasn't in the mood for it, he nodded and smiled at the luxury of the surroundings.

Room 323 stood at the end of the corridor, beckoning to him. He approached slowly, still racking his brains trying to place Jennifer Sandringham, the client. He wasn't a big movie buff; he'd rather listen to a good rock band play. Even so, he pretty much recognized most A-List celebrities; at least, the sort of international stars who could afford to pay for a place like this. He should have looked her up on the 'net, but he'd been much more interested in trying to track down Kelly instead. Kelly was the only woman on his mind right now, had been from the moment he met her.

He rapped on the door. No answer, so he rapped again. He reached into the inside pocket of his leather jacket and checked the address. The scrap of paper Daniel had scribbled the instructions down on definitely stated Room 323. He tried the handle and the door opened.

"Hello, is anybody home?"

No response. He stood in the open doorway scanning the room, a reception area to a full suite of rooms by the looks of it. There was a window at the far end and doors to the left and right, both closed. In the center of the space stood a fancy table, dominated by an explosion of flowers in a vase. A small envelope was propped against the display, and his name was scrawled across it. Apparently, he was in the right place.

He shut the door and walked over to the table, dumping his backpack on the floor. He picked up the envelope, turned it in his hands and lifted it to his nose. Beneath the smell of flowers from the display, he smelled a more exclusive scent. "The lady has expensive tastes."

He tried again to place the woman's name. Where was she anyway? He opened the envelope and pulled out a small white card.

When you're ready, come into the bedroom. Whatever happens, remember that you have signed a contract to be at my beck and call, all night long . . . and Tommy Sampson has a reputation to keep. Tommy Sampson never lets a client down . . .

Tommy stared at the card, rereading it with a frown. He'd felt uncomfortable about that clause in the contract, and now it was being emphasized. What the hell was this about? He flipped the card over. There was nothing on the back. Dropping the card on the table, he glanced at the two doors facing each other on either side of him.

As he contemplated them, he heard a key turning in the door behind him.

He turned, expecting someone to walk in. But no. He heard the faint sound of footsteps and laughter disappearing away down the corridor. "What the fuck?"

He crossed the room and tried the handle. The door that he had come through was now locked, with no sign of a key anywhere inside the reception area. He glared at it. Someone was having a joke at his expense, and he didn't like it.

He walked over to the door on the left, knocked, and entered. It opened onto a sitting room with low-slung leather sofas arranged around a marble coffee table. The room also had a wet bar, entertainment center, and a selection of faux-fur cushions and rugs draped across the chairs and floor. The décor instantly made him think of sex, and that did not lie easily with his current confusion about the setup. He ran a finger inside his collar, which suddenly felt tight and restrictive.

At my beck and call . . .

That suggestive phrase in the contract and the note kept echoing around his brain, unnerving him. Why the hell had he signed something so out of the ordinary? *Because you were too busy thinking about Kelly, that's why.*

"The bedroom," he murmured to himself. The note had read "When you're ready, come into the bedroom." *Shit.* Some mad woman wanted him in her bedroom and had him locked in, both physically and contractually. This was a big mistake. Daniel must have misunderstood what the woman was after. He really did not need this hassle now. He had enough of a woman issue to deal with, trying to track Kelly down, without adding some deluded celebrity into the mix.

Come into the bedroom . . .

She obviously thought . . . He swallowed. She obviously thought she'd hired a man for all her whims, and satisfying her in the bedroom department was a whim he had no intention of fulfilling. "I'll give Daniel hell."

Once he explained the mistake and got the hell out of here, his agent was in big trouble. Not to mention Jay. It was his so-called friend who'd gotten the wrong end of the stick here. But first he had to find the client and explain. He was tempted to call reception or—better still—just kick the door down and walk out, but he was a professional. This Jennifer woman needed to understand he was a trained security man, a bodyguard, and a roadie, not a fuckin' gigolo. The very thought of it made his hackles rise.

Dreading what he might find, he braced himself, stormed back through the reception area and opened the second door without knocking. The room was in darkness apart from the bed area, which was lit by fancy red lamps that seemed to be built into the headboard. They cast what was supposedly a seductive glow over black and red bed coverings. Tommy broke into a cold sweat. It looked like something from a Valentine's Day card, a heart-shaped bed with some sort of tentlike fabric hanging over it, like a harem. Thankfully, there wasn't anyone in the damn bed. He steeled himself and stepped into the room.

"Look, lady, there's been some sort of a mistake here."

He heard the sound of wicked chuckling in the darkness, then the door slammed shut behind him.

"What the fuck?" He went to turn on his heel, but not quickly enough. He was kicked in the back of the knees, buckling him. As he staggered forward, a hand pushed him in the small of the back. He lurched in the direction of the bed, which he cursed at as he collapsed onto it. The air whooshed from his lungs as he hit the surface. Inhaling, he got a face full of satin.

Lifting his head, swaying, he blinked and gathered himself, then someone or some*thing* leaped onto his back, snatching at his arms and locking them together at the small of his back. He felt fingers wrapping around his wrists.

Scowling and cursing, Tommy pulled his hands free, clambering up the bed, trying to break loose. *The thing*, whatever the hell it was, grunted and leaped, snatched hold of his belt, and hung on. The more he lurched away, the more his belt tightened on his hips and *the thing* jerked him back. His jeans were halfway down his arse and he felt sharp nails biting into his buttocks.

Shit, not only is she a complete maniac, she's a freakin' man-eater.

He'd heard stories about stuff like this, about men hired for sex. He'd read about them in those dodgy Sunday newspapers. But Tommy Sampson wasn't going to be a victim of some demented celebrity, left tied to a bed for some maid to find, no way. *Get a grip man*, he told himself. She was fast, and she was strong, but she was a woman.

He rolled onto his back, flipping them both over, and snatched at her hand where it was locked on to his belt. "Excuse me, but *I'm* the security person here. *I'm* supposed to protect *you* from people like *you*."

He gripped her by the wrists and hauled her physically up and onto his chest, pulling her closer into the lamplight to get a look at her.

She wriggled and hissed, her body sleek and lissome as a cat being held against its will, thick, dark hair flashing across her face and hiding her features. "Let me go," she demanded.

He opened his mouth to deny her, and then suddenly got a glimpse of her face, froze, and stared. "Kelly?"

She glared back at him, eyes narrowed and mouth pursed as if she was annoyed he'd thwarted her attack.

Despite his confusion, he broke into a grin. He couldn't help it. It was Kelly, it was really her. And she was looking really sexy in the hazy red light, dressed in some sort of fancy black underwear beneath a robe. The entire outfit was see-through, which made it very hard to concentrate on anything other than what was under it.

She wriggled free. "Yes, Kelly. Get used to it. You're here for the night, Buddy. I bought your time and you're all mine."

"You're Jennifer Sandringham?"

"Jennifer Sandringham is my great aunt, a blue-haired spinster from Northampton who spends most of her days complaining to the council about local affairs. I borrowed her name. It's me you have to answer to." She smiled then, and it was thoroughly bad.

The pulse in his groin started to beat hard. "I knew something wasn't right about this setup."

"And you walked right into it."

He lifted his eyebrows at her, grinning. "You went to a hell of a lot of trouble. You should have said you wanted another round. I'd have been happy to oblige."

She glared at him, as if annoyed. "I would have done, if you hadn't abandoned me in a hotel room."

His smile faded. She was angry. "I didn't abandon you. I mean, I did, but that's what I thought you wanted. I thought you were just out for a one-nighter. I thought you were after Clayton, that I was second choice."

She paused, staring at him in surprise, then gathered herself. "It would have been nice if you'd asked."

He barely registered that she'd gotten her hands on his wrists again. "It wasn't like that, and I'm sorry. Besides, I had to leave. My sister had her baby early, and I wanted to go over to the hospital to be with them. I should have woken you, but I didn't. I came back and you'd gone. I've been trying to find you all week. Do you know how many Kellys there are in London?"

She looked surprised, and stared at him silently for a moment. "You came back?"

He nodded. "I've been trying to track you down ever since. You didn't give me your last name."

"No, I didn't."

He thought she was softening, but then she flicked her hair back and grabbed his wrists back into her grasp. Jerking his arms straight, she held on to him.

He shook his head, laughing in disbelief. "How did you get to be so strong?"

"Hard work and a competitive nature." She clambered to her knees. "A liking for adventure sports." She flexed, her body rippling provocatively, agile as a feline. "I was the Southern Counties female canoeing champion title holder for two years running."

She climbed over him and straddled his hips. "I jog daily. I've placed in the London Marathon in the top one thousand every year since I started." She moved her hands up from his wrists, never breaking contact with him, and pinned his arms down with her hands locked around her biceps. "Oh, and I work in a gym, keeping shifty men like you in good shape."

"The moment I saw you I thought you'd make a great gym partner." He grinned. "But . . . 'shifty'? That's not very complimentary. Especially coming from a woman who just knocked the knees out from under me. If there was any shifty behavior here, that was it."

"I'm not here to pay you compliments, I'm here to return a favor." Mischief glinted in her eyes.

He wasn't sure what she meant, but he could barely focus on what she was saying. She'd tracked him down. His ego was swelling by the moment, and that wasn't all. With her sitting across his hips, pinning him down, looking so sexy, he was already getting hard.

She gave him a slow, hungry, once-over, her gaze lingering. "Are you ready for a really stiff workout, Tommy?"

His brain turned to mush. His dick did the reverse. Her sassy, suggestive smile made his balls ache. She had that mischievous look in her eye, her lips parted while she moved her crotch suggestively over him.

"Oh yes."

"Up for a challenge, huh?" She drew his hands to her body, putting them on her breasts.

He molded the satin-covered flesh with his hands, his focus shifting. She looked so damn good, like a fantasy come true. He couldn't wait to be inside her, to fuck her, fast, and then again, real slow.

She took one hand in hers, pulled it away, and kissed his fingertips, stroking his forearm, taking one finger in her mouth.

"Oh, yes, that's good." He moved his free hand into her cleavage, stroking her there, imagining his dick there. She was moving in and out of the shadows, and all he could focus on was her crotch rubbing against him, and her breast in his hand. It wasn't until she moved that hand too, and he automatically tried to use the other, that he found he couldn't. She had tethered it to the headboard and out to the side. Glancing over, he saw that a line of shiny, twisted black stuff extended from the headboard to his wrist, where it was tied tightly around his wrist. "What the hell is that?"

She'd swayed to the other side. "Bondage tape."

Bondage? "Wait a minute—"

"Too late, you're mine now, all mine." She leaned back, smiling at her handiwork. She'd gotten the other one tied too.

"Kelly?" He flexed his arms, tugged. The tape stretched marginally, but seemed to twist and tighten too. There were maybe ten inches of tape up to where she'd looped and tied it to the headboard, but it wasn't enough for his liking. He was ready to do whatever she wanted, but he'd never been tied up before.

"I'm quite sure you could break free, but I'd like to remind you at this point that you signed a contract to be at my beck and call."

She was right. "Yes. I see." What the hell had he let himself in for? "You don't need to tie me up, believe me. I'm very willing."

"Oh, but I do need to tie you up. You were very rude to me, so it's my turn to punish you."

The idea of being punished by her, sexually, almost won out in the battle of body over mind. Yes, he wanted to know. He might not have been tied up before, but a dark sense of curiosity was fast creeping up on him. His brain, however, was still clinging to a shred of logic, and wanted to challenge her some more on a different matter. "Is that all this is, punishment?"

He didn't believe her, and he chuckled softly, eyeing her in mock accusation. "I mean, we've seen each other two weekends in a row, doesn't that imply we're in some sort of relationship?"

"No." She glared at him. "I'm an independent woman. I only need men for one thing." She returned her attention to his body and opened his shirt, clawing his chest, her nails raking over it, sending slivers of twisted pleasure under his skin.

At that point, his brain surrendered, handing over full control of the logic center to his bodily desires. "Oh yes, play rough, Kelly, play rough," he challenged.

She flashed him a dark look. Shuffling down his body, she undid his belt and fly. He shut his eyes and thanked the heavens. She was going to ride him; he'd been fantasizing about this all week.

She took his dick out, stroking it, sensitizing it. It was rock hard and ready to be inside her sweet cunt. She dropped down and ran her tongue over the head, tantalizing him.

Oh yes, that's good.

Taking the head of his dick in her mouth she moved her tongue against the underside. She heard him growl, and she moved up to look into his eyes. "I hope you've got lots of stamina, Tommy. You're going to need it tonight."

There was a threat and a promise there, and it did bad things to him. "I've been building stamina all week, fantasizing about this moment."

She smiled then, but her eyelids lowered, as if she didn't want him to know that his remark had pleased her. She was a strange woman, but he was finding a way in through her shell, and he was going to pursue it.

"I'm going to undress you now." She locked eyes with him. "And I want you to remember I bought your time. I don't want you trying to break free."

He nodded down at his erection. "I'm not going anywhere until I've been inside you."

She gave a little self-satisfied smile, and it held a dark secret. He sensed it and it made his blood pound. What was she intending to do?

She undid his shirt, leaving it open, baring his chest. She turned her attention to his boots, taking them off, along with his socks, and then she tackled his jeans, hauling them and his Jockeys down his thighs.

Licking her lips, she smiled at him. "I'm fascinated by your body. You're a prize specimen, Tommy Sampson."

Pride plumed in his chest. His spine straightened, his shoulders going back as she moved around the bed, admiring him.

When she got closer, he longed to reach out for her. "I can smell you, let me see you."

He jerked his chin, trying to indicate she take off the robe and get closer. He couldn't reach her, and that gutted him.

"I'm in charge here."

Don't speak. She wants to be in charge. Whatever she wanted, as long as he got to be inside her.

She moved away and began to take off her robe. He watched as it slipped from her shoulders. Her body looked glorious in the red lamplight, a fantasy come true. She pulled her bra straps down her shoulders, reached back and undid it. It fell away, leaving her breasts bared to his eyes.

She hardly seemed to be aware of him watching as she put her thumbs inside her panties and lowered them down her thighs. No showing off, no need for attention. It was as if she were just undressing at the end of a day. Somehow, that was sexier to him than if she'd done a full-on striptease. He had the feeling that he'd be running the scene in his mind over and over again.

She walked back toward him.

"Ride me, please ride me." He couldn't help it, the words were out.

"Tut tut, Tommy." She shook her head, her hands on her hips. They jutted forward, her posture suddenly self-assured and powerfully feminine.

That old *Modesty Blaise* book cover came back into his head at that moment.

"How many times do I need to tell you? You are here for my pleasure. I'm going to do to you"—she ran one finger from his hip to his shoulder—"everything you did to me, but with *style*."

What did she mean? The way she said "style" daunted him for some reason.

"Can you remember what you did to me?" She looked fiery, lust-filled.

His heart was beating hard; he was getting desperate to fuck her. He was so hard it was becoming painful. He nodded, the realization hitting him. "I punished you, physically."

I spanked her. Shit. She was taking control in the most extreme way. *If anyone can, she can*, a devilish thought suggested. Yes, and he wanted to know if she could, he wanted to experience her domination. His dick was up against his belly, distended and hot. "Give me all you've got, Kelly," he rasped.

She smiled, her hand resting briefly on his shoulder, acknowledging his consent. "Roll over," she instructed, pushing his hips and forcing him up and into a kneeling position.

As he moved, the two twines of black tape crossed, twisting tight like a tourniquet. Resting on his fists, his hands were now locked together within the bindings. He felt vulnerable, naked as he was but for his open shirt, while she stood over him. With his head on one side, he watched as she reached for the bedside table where there was a vanity bag he hadn't noticed before.

Reaching inside, she pulled out various objects and dropped them on the bed. She lifted a small, black one, about eight inches long. At first he couldn't make out what it was, but she picked it up turned it in her hands and then pulled on one end. It was some sort of telescopic baton. He looked at the small rubber paddle on one end and realized. She really meant it when she said she was going to do everything he did to her, "in style."

"Now I get to have my fun," she whispered, with a dark promise, stroking his head as she bent over him.

She truly was a wild woman, but right now, she was a wild woman in control. Her power had him firmly in its grip, and she wasn't even touching him yet. He could barely breathe. His dick was pounding, his balls tight against it. His arse twitched as he tried to anticipate what it might feel like. He watched as she closed in on him, her eyes narrowed and her mouth gently smiling, as she swatted the baton through the air, testing it out.

Without warning, she homed in on her target and he felt the first swat of the whip across his buttocks. The sting reverberated through him, jolting through his joints, making him hot and cold all at once.

She delivered several more swats, then knelt one knee on the bed, reached her free hand under him and clasped his dick. She worked his shaft while she let rip with another flick of her whip across the back of his thighs.

His vision blurred. He closed his eyes tightly. Sweat broke out on his forehead. It was too much. He was going to come, fast. Too fast.

She delivered two more swats. He was so close. Then, suddenly, he felt her hand stroking his back, soothing him, and some iota of control returned, the orgasm retreating a tad, enough for him to breathe. She was still working his dick, moving it in the most mesmerizing way.

He sensed her moving, looked around but too late to see what she'd done. Then he felt something cold sliding down in between his buttocks. Lube.

His thighs tightened, his body rocking on his knees. The way she was working his erection, he could barely focus, but then he felt it, a slim butt plug easing into his passage. Sensation roared up his spine. His knees slid from under him. He heard her laugher echoing around him, as he slid flat to the bed.

"What the hell are you doing to me?" he croaked.

He couldn't comprehend it, and the words escaped him as he tried to understand the torrent of sensation he was experiencing at her hands. He struggled, but his mind was mush.

Her hand was still wrapped around him and he lifted his hips automatically, allowing her movement. As he did, the plug hit home.

"Oh, oh, fuck, fuck," he shouted. Ecstasy hit him hard. He spurted in her hand, his arsehole tight around the intrusion, his buttocks flexing, working it hard on instinct alone. He lost touch with the room, with everything except her. *Kelly.* Her name was in his mind as he came.

"Yes, you naughty boy. I'm here." Her tone was soothing and he let it run over him, surfacing.

Must have said her name aloud, he realized, his mind barely functioning. He was flat to the bed. The plug was gone.

As he regained his faculties, he heard her leave and then return from the bathroom. Then her hands were on his back and stroking him. She forced him over onto his back, untwisting the tape, and climbed over him, straddling his waist. Kneeling up, her body was taut and beautiful in the light. As she looked down at him, her eyes glinted. Her nipples jutted out between her fingers as she molded her breasts in her hands, squeezing them.

"Oh god," he murmured, swallowing, looking up at her towering over him. He was so aroused that he was hard again already, even though he'd come. He was praying, willing her to sit on him. His erection jerked up behind her buttocks, but she ignored it.

Instead, she shut her eyes, reached for her pussy and started to touch herself in front of him, just inches away from his face. Her fingers opened up her lips, squeezed either side of her clit. He couldn't reach her, but he could see her and her scent filled his senses. *Shit, she is trying to drive me insane.*

"Why don't you let me do that, please?" His urge to get her back—and how—was growing.

Her eyes opened, and she was restraining a smile as her fingers slicked in and out. She looked like a dark goddess, so powerful and confident.

He pulled his hands as wide apart as he could within the restraints. "Come on, Kelly. Sit on my face. Let me taste you. You know you want to."

"I'm in charge here." She slapped his cheek. The sting seemed to commute directly to the base of his spine, his tight balls, and his sensitive cock. She clambered over his shoulders, her thighs spreading on either side of his head, her feet latched over his shoulders as she lowered her pussy to his mouth.

"Oh yes," he breathed the words over her skin, before he sank his mouth into it. Her flesh was warm, damp, and full. He was ready for more, and he was almost willing to beg, but he gave her his full attention, running his tongue around the intimate grooves of her pussy.

She moaned aloud, snatched at the headboard as her body wavered.

Her torso rose up above him, her breasts jutting, her hands gripping the bed for balance. He pushed his tongue into her hole and his mouth filled with her juices. She cried out with pleasure, as if it was already too much for her.

A victory cry roared up inside him, because he was hungry for her, and he was only just getting started.

Chapter Six

Kelly had to hang on to the headboard to steady herself. She'd barely gotten a grip on what was going on, the sense of power she was experiencing acting like some heady narcotic in her blood. Now his tongue and mouth were doing the most outrageous things to her: teasing, stroking, sucking—all of it wiring her into his mouth as if it were a divining rod.

He dipped his head back, breathed on her sensitive skin, making her shiver. "You taste so good, I could eat you forever."

His words made her weak, and she swayed.

He gave a subtle laugh, breathing on her skin again, and then pounced back in.

Desperate for her release, she began responding to him, her hips moving of their own accord. The rough touch of his stubble brushing against her perineum was like a trigger point, hitting over and over. He moved faster, his tongue stroking in around her labia then lapping at her clit, before roving down and pushing inside her sex.

"Oh, oh, Tommy," she cried, on the brink.

He bit into her gently, halting her, drawing out the pleasure, then alternating fast and slow strokes, sucking and nibbling. He was eating her up, his mouth moving from her dripping hole, back up to her clit, where he nursed it in his mouth, sending wave after wave of hot pleasure through her groin.

As she got closer to her peak, her hips rolled back and forth in time with his strokes, reaching out for the orgasm. His tethered arms squeezed against the underside of her thighs, his shoulders hard under her buttocks. He was nurturing her, encouraging her, and that made her melt. She almost gave in and went for his cock, but wouldn't let herself—not yet.

He ran his teeth gently over her clit and that was it, her sex clenched, went into spasm. Shuddering, her body quaked with intensity. Liquid dribbled down her thighs and onto his face.

"Easy, girl." His voice brought her back.

She loved it when he said that, it made her feel warm inside, warm in a different way. She pulled herself together; she didn't want him to know she was ready to undo him and be held, be loved. She was fighting it hard, and she shuffled back, wiping his face with trembling fingers. Dropping down, she kissed him.

He reached for her kiss, his tongue eager for her, and she returned it briefly, before moving away. She picked up her robe and headed for the bathroom. She heard him call her name in a querying tone, and felt guilty. "Give me a minute, I won't be long."

Closing the door behind her, she leaned back against it, shutting her eyes. She was starting to get a grip, thank god. She'd got so wrapped up in their coupling, she'd kind of lost her focus. Her blood was still racing, though, her sex on fire, liquid heat running down her thighs. She rubbed them together sending an after tremor of pleasure through her body. It had been so hot, his large masculine body bound for her. The power of controlling him had made her wetter than she'd ever been. And he'd been willing, egging her on. This was supposed to be about getting revenge, she mused. He was enjoying it. *Pervert.*

She gave an incredulous laugh, opened her eyes, and went over to the fancy vanity unit to check her makeup. The mirror was surrounded by built-in lights, the fixtures luxurious. She'd treated herself to the robe and undies; new cosmetics, some hot lipstick and some perfume she thought would match the surroundings. This was her treat, and she was enjoying every moment of it.

Her own mischievous smile empowered her again. She reapplied her lipstick, a shade she thought would be better named "hussy red" than "pillar box," checked her profile, and took a deep breath as she left the bathroom.

What a sight. He looked like some fantasy painting by Boris Vallejo, one of her favorite artists. Vallejo depicted men of power and muscle in fantasy scenarios, and Tommy looked that way now, like a mighty warrior bound and imprisoned.

She could have admired him all evening, but she still had an agenda—and a point to prove. She reached over to the bedside cabinet and opened the drawer. Pulling out the CD Clayton had signed for her earlier that week she waved it in front of his face. "This is what I wanted to see Clayton about, an autograph for my friend. None of you actually believed a word I said."

He gave a soft sigh. "I'm sorry. I can see it's the truth, and that it really matters to you."

"Of course it does."

"You have to admit, you did look as if you were up to something dodgy, shooting out of a private dressing room, don't you think? If you'd been in my position, you'd have thought the very same thing."

She wriggled her shoulders. He was right, but she wanted him to believe her now, above all. "It's the assumption that annoys me. If you had believed me in the first place, maybe you wouldn't have abandoned me in a hotel room—"

"I didn't abandon you," he interrupted. "I came back."

I came back. ". . . and you wouldn't be in this situation."

"This 'situation' isn't so bad." He winked. "If I'd have believed you, and you'd gotten your autograph, I would have had no reason to spank you, my dear." He grinned at her, moving his arms and nodding at his tethering. "Now, why don't you untie me, and we can get down to something much more satisfying than arguing about how we met."

"Not so fast, buddy."

"Kelly . . ." There was a plea there now, and a frown had appeared on his forehead.

"I figured the pain of a sustained erection might be a punishment in a league of its own."

He stared at her, uncomprehending at first. Then his lips tightened. "You're probably right, but aren't you punishing yourself for the sake of punishing me? Don't you want to come again, and again? I can make you, you know I can."

Her sex clenched. She sighed audibly. "Oh, don't worry so."

She stroked his cheek, cupping it, and savoring the feel of it in her hand. "I'm not done with you yet."

She walked to the other side of the room where her underwear had landed. Pulling on her panties, she noticed his expression growing concerned.

"Where are you going? You're not going to leave me here are you?" Again he yanked on the tethering, but the PVC bondage tape just stretched and held tight, and it was the bed itself that rattled.

Luckily, she'd doubled the tape up; he was a big man to keep tied up with PVC. She couldn't help laughing. He'd begun to look quite panicked. She dawdled back to him. "I have champagne on ice next-door, and I'm going to order us some snacks. I want to keep your strength up."

"My strength is just fine. I've been building up reserves all week just thinking about you, now let me prove it."

His words secretly thrilled her, but she waved her hand around the room. "I spent my holiday fund on buying your time and renting this suite. I'm going to enjoy every moment of it . . . at my own pace."

His eyes narrowed. "I'll refund the fee, and I'll pay for the suite too, just untie me." He gazed at her longingly. "I want to get my hands on you and satisfy you properly."

She smiled. "All in good time."

As she left the bedroom, she patted the condoms in her robe pocket, and began humming the *Mission: Impossible* theme to herself, happily.

. . .

From the bed, Tommy could see across the reception area and through the doorway into the sitting room. Watching her sauntering back and forth was not helping his growing sense of frustration. He was seriously considering the possibility that this kind of restraint and endurance test could drive him insane. He'd be a happy man with her sitting on his face all night, as long as he could fuck her afterward. It was like an unfinished, mouthwatering meal. He'd had his appetizers and could see the main course on the plate; he was starving but he couldn't get to the damn thing.

She seemed to be taking great delight in wandering back and forth where he could see her, without acknowledging him. Earlier, when she'd strolled out of the bathroom looking like Modesty Blaise, his dick was up like a flagpole in an instant. Now he could hear her speaking on the phone, and it sounded like she was ordering food from room service.

Moments later, she walked across the hallway with an ice bucket and a bottle of champagne. She had a point about the suite. But when she untied him, he was going to screw her into the bed until she begged for mercy.

Before he had time to make any more plans along those lines, he heard a knock at the door and she walked out into reception, pulling a key from her robe pocket as she did, sparing him a smile as she passed.

He rolled his eyes, his ears pricking up as he heard a key in the door and voices. A moment later he saw her walk back into the sitting room. A uniformed member of staff followed with a food trolley, a man.

Shit. When the guy came back, he was almost certain to see him there. He tried to sit up on the bed, and then realized that made him even more noticeable. He could have torn himself free, but that wouldn't be playing the game, would it? He pressed his lips shut in grim determination, flattening himself against the bed as best he could, his eyes narrowed as he watched the doorway.

You've done this on purpose, you vixen.

A minute later the man emerged and skirted the table in the entrance hall, jolting to a halt when he looked into the bedroom.

Tommy tried to shut his eyes, but something in his nature made him peek with one eye. The guy straightened his bow tie, and thankfully, left. Not before smirking to himself, though. The news about the poor sod tied to the bed in Room 323 would soon be all over the hotel.

A couple of minutes later Kelly came back in. She reached over him, as if to undo his ties, but paused to stroke his jawline. As she did, her fingers brushed the underside of it.

Yet again, she had found his danger zone. He rolled his head from side to side, trapping her fingers against the pillow.

"What is it with you there?"

"It's sensitive."

Her eyes lit. "Oh right—it's an erogenous spot?" She stroked it again, and then her gaze lowered to his groin. "Oh, that is something." She gave a soft chuckle as his erection bounced high in response to her touch.

"Kelly, please. You are driving me mad here." He could smell her perfume, mixed with the underlying aroma of her release, and he was desperate to be inside her. He wanted to let loose and screw her into the bed. If she didn't actually untie him and let him act on it, insanity was a distinct possibility. "Please."

"Oh, I do love to hear a man begging, but you're just going to have to wait." She threw a chastising glance in the direction of his erection.

That disapproving look, whether in fun or not, did strange things to him. He shut his eyes tightly for a moment, to ground himself.

"Look at the state of you. I'm going to have to make you more respectable for our après-sex canapés and champagne."

He snorted. The idea of it, while he was in this state, was surreal.

"I'm going to untie you, but you better be good." She unraveled his tethers, keeping them in her hand. "Sit on the edge of the bed."

He obliged, watching as she pulled his jeans back on, hauling them up to his knees. She nodded her head, indicating he get up.

He stood, watching as she twisted the strands of bondage tape together to make a lead.

"Versatile stuff," he commented.

"I told you last week I could make you my slave." She let the lead drop from her hand, and hauled his jeans up over his arse.

She knew he could escape. She was playing with him; maybe she wanted him to break free. The idea pleased him. "Right now it feels as if *you* are *my* slave—I've never been dressed by a woman before."

Humor flickered across her face. "You keep pushing the issue, don't you? I bought your time, get used to it. Anyway, I've never dressed a man before, but don't let it go to your head." He could see the laughter in her expression, even though she was trying to hide it.

"I'm playing your game, madam, but I could have you over on your back in a minute." He was hauling back his male urges to do just that, biding his time until he sensed it was what she really wanted.

"I know." She didn't bat an eyelid. "I'm the boss here. I just want to keep you as my slave for a little bit longer."

You can have me for as long as you like. He knew better than to say it aloud, though, but the urge to do so was there.

She reached for his fly, easing his cock inside his jeans with effort. She chuckled. "Getting this back in here reminds me of Clayton. When you came into the dressing room that night, you caught him in a similar situation."

He cringed, pushing the image out of his mind. "Oh, please, I'll never be able to look either of them in the eye again."

"Believe me, I was much more interested in you than the pair of them. I'd spotted you beforehand and admired your body."

Something swelled inside him. "I wish I'd known that last week."

She shrugged and fastened his shirt, slowly lingering over each button as if she was enjoying the task

Mention of Clayton and Jay reminded him of Jennifer Sandringham and the setup. "Wait a minute; it was Jay who gave you my agent's number. How in the hell did you get that out of him?"

"I shanghaied Clayton, kind of. He wasn't too pleased at first, but I convinced him."

She did the last button then lifted his lead, and twisted it to make it strong. "Come with me. Since you were such a good boy back there on the bed"—she reached to kiss his mouth, fleetingly— "I'll let you have some nibbles and champagne."

She winked and walked off.

He had no other choice but to follow. At first it felt awkward. He felt like a lumbering fool. Then he looked at the elegant lines of her body moving inside that sheer robe of hers as she walked in front of him. Her posture was perfect; her chin lifted high, a slight smile on her face when she glanced back at him. She was amazing.

He had the urge to get down on his hands and knees and beg her for another taste. He wanted to kiss her from her ankles to the crease beneath her buttocks, and then tongue her inside. *Let her take charge*, he reminded himself. *Yes, until later.*

In the sitting room, she'd set the food out on the marble coffee table; the champagne was open and poured. She'd put rock music on the stereo and arranged two of the fur rugs on the floor, one white, one black. She urged him toward them.

He dropped down, immediately wondering what her naked body would look like against the black fur.

Before she joined him, she pulled a condom out of her pocket. Turning it in her fingers, she made sure he was watching, and then she put it on the tray with the food, on the far side out of his immediate reach.

He shook his head, smiling. "You're such a tease."

"Consider it a promise. I didn't want you to think I was being too cruel."

"Maybe just cruel enough . . . ?"

Her eyes sparkled.

He looked up at her, watched the shift of her breasts under the robe.

She noticed and sat down nearby, smiling to herself. "So, you're an uncle?"

"Just, yes. I've got one sister, Carol, and it's her first. Although she claims she wants a half dozen. God help us all. I think she means it."

"You're a family man?" There was wary curiosity in her expression.

"Never really thought about it, but I guess so. Our parents retired to Spain, so I watch out for her. Jim, Carol's husband, he's a great guy, and a real computer genius, but he has no business sense." He winked.

She nodded, but her eyelids were lowered, hiding her reaction from him. It was as if she wanted to know, but didn't.

"So . . . I take care of that side of things for them. We share a business, a computer business. Mail order and shop. Our parents are flying in soon enough though, to meet their first grandchild."

She had knelt up and was moving dishes about on the coffee table, for no real reason. Had he said too much?

"What about you? Family?"

She shook her head and put a plate of snacks in between them. "I share a flat with two friends. My mother lives on the south coast. She has a guest house there. That's it." She reached for a glass and swigged champagne.

He could tell she didn't want him to pry any further, so he turned his attention to the food. "Looks good." He wasn't hungry at all, but he knew she'd have to feed him and that was going to be something.

She nodded, pleased, and lifted the flute of champagne to his lips. It was chilled and delicious, hitting the back of his throat in a flavor-filled froth. She'd spared no expense, and she said she worked in a gym. Could she really afford this? She said it was her holiday money. She wanted this badly enough, he didn't miss that. But he was going to make Daniel pay her back.

She fed him asparagus sticks and caviar on delicate, thinly sliced toasts. "Good?" she asked.

"Oh, yes." It was all very luxurious, but he barely noticed. His concentration was on her, her fingers at his mouth, her lips parting when he ate the food from her fingertips. It was erotic, with her so sexily dressed and that look of satisfaction she had about her. Sex made her look different. More relaxed maybe, or mellow.

And there was the fact that he kept getting flashes of her pussy through the transparent material of her panties, when her robe shifted. He could see the soft, dark hair at her groin. It drew his attention to the groove where he was longing to bury himself. She might have dressed him for "après-sex canapés," as she called it, but, as far as he was concerned, she was still dressed to be fucked— gloriously fucked.

The champagne seemed to kick in, and she sprawled out on the fur rug, lying on one side, her legs elegantly aligned, toes pointed, her ankle seeming to invite a kiss.

"You took a risk, setting this up," he said, suddenly curious.

The champagne had definitely gotten to her; her eyes had a dreamy look about them. "Yes, but if you'd walked out on me, I still had the suite to enjoy." She didn't seem surprised by his comment.

He supposed people remarked on her devil-may-care attitude a lot. "It was a crazy thing to do."

"Like I said before, life is short. I like to have fun." Her gaze ran over him. "Nothing to lose," she murmured.

"And everything to gain?" He chuckled.

She shook her head, not smiling. "Just nothing to lose. That's the way I like it."

The laughter faded on his lips. Why did that make his chest feel heavy? He sensed her creating distance between them again. She was wary, wary of getting close.

"But you came after me."

She stared at him for a long moment before she replied. "For one more night, Tommy, one more night."

"But you came after me," he insisted. She had to want more.

She reached over and silenced him with a kiss, but it was too late. He knew. She was as prickly as a wounded hedgehog, and she'd rolled into a ball so he couldn't pick her up. *Don't press her*, he warned himself. He felt something hankering inside him, though. Need. He wanted to carry her to the bed now, and every night. He wanted to keep her in his arms. Instead he returned her kiss and when she moved back to lie on her side again, he got to his knees and bent down to kiss her ankle, where it had attracted his attention earlier.

She gave a pleasured sigh, and he knew he was back on track. He stroked the top of her foot with one knuckle, his bound hands useless to do more. Tracing the curve of her calf muscle with his lips, he breathed across her skin. She trembled beneath him. He kissed the side of her knee, and then leaned over and tongued the back of it. Her hands clutched at the rug, her fingers so pale, digging in against the black fur.

Moving up her thighs, he breathed in the aroma of her pussy. It was intoxicating, so seductive to him. With his tethered hands, he traced the camber of her back, where it dipped and then flared at her hips. Her bottom was perfect, soft and firm. He bent his head and ran his tongue over the surface of her panties, gratified when he heard her give a whimper of frustration. She wanted it. So did he.

His dick was practically poking through his jeans, his lower back aching with restraint. He licked her belly, dipping into her navel and shuffling up on his knees to reach between her breasts, where her skin was salty. He took the rigid peak of one nipple, exploring its knotted surface with his tongue.

She was on her back and undulating against the rug, her body arching. Then her fingers moved to stroke his hair and when he glanced up he saw that she had lifted her head and was looking at him, her expression intense, her lips parted with anticipation.

He turned his face into her fingers and kissed them. "Untie me, please," he whispered. "I need to be inside you."

"Show me how much you want it," she whispered, propping herself up and nodding at his hands where they were bound.

He knelt up, lifted his wrists in front of his chest. Tensing his muscles, he pulled, stretching the tape beyond its capacity, ripping it and breaking free.

"Oh, Tommy." She took a deep intake of breath. She rolled flat onto her back, seeming to melt into the rug, her robe pooling around her. She was breathing heavily.

Pulling the stands of tape free, he grabbed at his shirt buttons, popping several of them in his haste. She watched as he threw off the shirt and leaned over, lifting the condom from the tray. He unzipped his jeans, took his dick in his hand and rolled the condom on, her gaze making him proud.

"I've longed for this," he whispered, as his mouth descended toward hers again. He peeled her panties down her legs and she slipped the robe off her shoulders. He hauled her body to his. She tilted her head back, her eyes heavy with desire, fingers entwined in his hair. She was all woman, and he wanted to be inside her. Her lips were eager and moist, parting readily to take his tongue. She caressed his neck, and then slid one hand down to feel the muscles on his chest.

"I want you, Tommy, and I . . ." Her voice faltered. "Hurry, I don't want to waste a moment." Her hips moved against him, her hand reaching for his sheathed erection, stroking it.

"Neither do I." He groaned. With her hand on his dick like that, the need to be inside her was growing ever more urgent. He climbed over her open thighs, his dick seeking her out. Rising up on his arms, he paused briefly to look at the need in her face. Her eyes were bright and feverish, and her thighs drew up around his flanks.

"I thought about this all week . . . is it such a crime to want you?" He lifted her chin as he spoke and looked deep into her eyes. She shook her head.

"Tommy," she moaned, a plea in her voice, hands clutching at him when she felt his dick nudging into her.

With one strong thrust, he was buried to the hilt inside her, and her body closed tightly around him. *Oh, that felt so good.* She clutched him so invitingly, her cunt so hot and slippery. He groaned aloud, thrusting deep against her, reaching for each demand of her body on his. Her hands were on his back, pulling him harder against her, a pant freeing from her throat each time their movements met.

He moved her legs higher, and she latched them over his shoulders, bending her under him. He felt how her body molded inside, how it reacted to him, how each thrust reverberated through the tender, sensitive flesh of her cunt.

She rolled her head, looking away, but he drew her back with one finger against her chin, locking eyes with her. His thighs trembled with effort.

She struggled with eye contact, it was almost too much to ask of her, but he could see that she wanted to do it, as he much as he wanted her to.

"Kelly," he whispered, slowing his movements inside her. He paused midsentence to pull out and thrust deeper. He groaned.

She nodded. "Now."

He was determined to stay with her. When he felt her jolt and quiver from deep between her thighs, he was harnessed to her and her moment. She was running eager hands over his shoulders, pulling at him. She cried out, her fingers gripping his shoulders tightly, her cunt clutching over and over.

The climax barreled through him, tensing his every muscle, his body seizing, his dick lurching. He roared aloud, letting some of the tension escape that way. Gasping for breath, he blinked to regain his focus and saw her looking up at him still.

As the climax subsided, he shifted his hands on the floor, realigned himself, one hand going to her leg against his neck, stroking it, turning into it and kissing it, lovingly.

"So good, you feel so good," he murmured. "Oh, Kelly . . ."

She wormed from his grasp, closing on him instead. Rolling him onto his back, she kissed him hard, stopping the words he might have said.

Chapter Seven

Don't look back.

Kelly stood at the bedroom door, both hands against it. She was dressed and ready to go—with all her fancy underwear and cosmetics in her backpack—but something inside her felt as if it were being torn apart. All she had to do was leave. He was asleep. She just had to walk through the door, and she'd fulfill her quest for revenge. He'd wake up alone, just like she'd done the week before. The victory felt strangely hollow now, though. It had been so good the night before, that's why.

When she'd finally let him break free and take her, it had been the most intense thing she'd ever experienced. He hadn't let her look away, maintaining eye contact the whole while. She'd never made love like that before, and that's what it was: making love.

I've never actually "made love" before, she realized, and she was already craving more of it.

She fought the rising urge to return to the bed, to snuggle in against him and wake him with a kiss. They could share breakfast in bed, make love again. *You don't need men*, she reminded herself, *only for one thing*. The fact that he was so good at it was no reason to stay with him. *Don't be weak*. She rested her forehead against the door.

He will only hurt you.

That did it. Taking a deep breath, she moved one hand to the door handle, and turned it. The door clicked open. For one, brief moment, she paused, hoping that the sound had woken him, that he'd call her back. But all was quiet, save the sound of his breathing as he slept. Opening the door, she shook off her silly doubts and went through it.

Tommy stirred, yawning and blinking into the narrow line of sunlight that shone into the room. It took him a few moments to work out where he was, and as he did so he had a strong feeling of déjà vu.

Just like last week all over again, he thought, with a smile. Except the curtains had been completely shut last night. Kelly must have opened them. Moving, he realized he was alone in the bed. Sitting up, he pushed back the covers, ruffled his hair, and glanced round. The bathroom door was open. She wasn't in there. Perhaps she'd gone to order breakfast. He reached over and put his hand into the soft dent where her body had lain in the bed. It was cold.

That's when it dawned on him. She'd left him alone in the hotel room, just as he had done to her the week before. He knew she hadn't intended for it to be more than another night, but he'd been too wrapped up in the sex the night before to figure what might happen next. He wasn't overly surprised, though, not anymore. He was getting to know her, no matter how hard she tried to keep him out. He noticed a small white envelope on her pillow, marked with his name. "So you got me back, did you?"

Yes, but she had left a note. Being the sort who was into games and one-upmanship, she would, though, wouldn't she? He shook his head, but he couldn't help being amused. He might have known; he was learning fast. Second-guessing her would be easier the next time. And there would be a next time; he was going to make sure of that. She had played him at his game, so he would play her at hers.

He picked up the envelope, turned it over and pulled out the card.

Now you know how it feels.

That was it, no other comments, it wasn't even signed, so he still didn't know her last name. Smiling wryly to himself, he realized she'd kept him awake until well past dawn, making sure he was worn out, so that he wouldn't wake when she slipped off. She'd planned this all along, the vixen. Although he supposed he deserved it, at least in her eyes. The way she'd forced him to look at the autograph showed him that much. Everything she'd said, she'd meant. She wanted him to believe her, stubborn and determined; she really had something to prove. And so did he, now.

He'd have to work a lot harder to show her he hadn't wanted to walk away from her. If he'd known she was really interested in him at the outset, they'd still be making the furniture rattle in that very first hotel room, let alone this one. She wanted more, whether she admitted it or not. This hadn't just been about revenge. She'd enjoyed every minute as much as he had. Whatever reason she had for being so bloody prickly, he wasn't going to let her get away.

Running the card against his nose, he took another breath of that scent she'd been wearing. He rested back against the pillows, dropping the card on his chest. Breakfast in bed would have been good. Feeding her tidbits while she looked at him with those strange eyes of hers. He supposed he should be grateful she hadn't left him tied to the bed for the maid to find. He scanned the room. No sign of the bondage tape.

Did you keep that for a souvenir, or for another time, Kelly? He groaned, his mind running over the events of the night before, savoring every filthy moment. She'd been a wildcat in bed the weekend before, but seeing her take charge like that last night was something else. She'd used him so thoroughly. He'd never experienced such intense sexuality—such confident domination—in a woman before. Oh, he'd played at it with others, but with Kelly she'd got so far into the role-playing it had consumed her. And him too.

He ran his hand over his dick, half risen. He still tasted her in his mouth. He wanted to taste her in his mouth again. *And again.* Idly stroking himself, he shut his eyes and pictured her over him, her taut body towering over him while she lowered her pussy to his mouth. He'd been hard as rock, his balls aching, when he filled his mouth with her, his tongue exploring every soft, damp inch, devouring her pussy.

His dick went rigid in his palm. Her kinky sex games would haunt him, and she knew it. He chuckled softly. She was a vixen, a devious, scheming, crazy vixen—and he loved it. If she wanted to play games, he was definitely up for it.

Kelly shut the front door behind her and dropped her backpack on the sofa, unsure whether she was glad to be home or not. Jojo wasn't around; her parents had taken her off to a cottage in the country for the weekend for a change of scenery.

The faint sound of classical music came from the vicinity of Helen's bedroom. She'd be in bed with the Sunday papers, a large mug of percolated coffee, and the classical station on her stereo. It was Helen's once-a-week effort at being informed and intellectual. The rest of the week she played loud rock music and drank instant.

Kelly was glad Helen didn't appear. She wasn't in the mood to speak to anyone right then. Reaching into her bag, she pulled out the CD that Clayton had autographed for Jojo. It had served one purpose, now it would serve another. She went to her friend's room, where she lifted one of Jojo's cuddly toys from the shelf, and sat it on the bed with the CD propped between its paws. That would bring a smile to her face. "Mission accomplished," she murmured to herself.

When she got inside her own sanctuary, she looked around as if with fresh eyes. It was so different from the exclusive hotel suite of the night before, but she wouldn't want to live in a place like that all the time. Somewhere in between would be nice. She made a mental note to invest in a couple of framed prints and some faux-fur scatter rugs next payday.

She headed for the bed, taking off her clothes on the way. She didn't think she would be able to sleep, her mind was whirring and her body was suffering the kind of obsessive sexual awareness that came from two all-night sessions that blew the mind. But she was physically tired, and it was the logical thing to do.

It had been so hard to leave him, she mused. All she'd wanted to do was snuggle up against him, enjoy the feeling of his body next to hers, until he awoke. It was one of the hardest things she'd ever done, making herself turn away in order to complete her mission. But it was done and over with. Now she was home and she had to get on with her life.

As she dropped her jeans and T-shirt onto the floor she caught sight of herself in the full-length mirror on her wardrobe. Startled, she paused and stepped closer, examining her reflection with curiosity. She looked sated, oh yes, but a bit shell-shocked too. Her hair was a bed-tousled mess, her skin glowed, and her eyes looked full of hidden secrets. On her body, she could see evidence of the sheer physicality of their passion—a kiss bruise on her neck and chest, and a faint bruise on the back of her hip where he'd rolled her across the floor, staying inside her the whole while. Thinking about the way he'd been, so demanding, so determined—even in bondage—her head dropped back and she sighed. He was a force of nature, and he'd hit her hard.

She turned this way and that, looking at her profile. Undoing her bra, she let it drop to the floor. There was definitely something different about her reflection, but she couldn't work out what it was. Moving closer still, she pushed her hair back from her forehead and scrutinized her face. Her lips looked swollen, slightly bruised. Maybe that was it. Her hand instinctively went over her lace-covered mons; it was bruised and sensitive too. She smiled, remembering. As she did she noticed something else. A slight sense of sadness in her eyes, perhaps?

"You really like him," she said to herself, with a wry smile. *That's what it is.* She hadn't looked that way the night before. It was as if the sense of loss had suddenly appeared in the cold light of day, when she had woken and known she had to sneak out without waking him or saying good-bye, to complete her plan.

Stepping away from the mirror, she threw back the quilt and flung herself on the bed. Lying on her back, she shut her eyes. The sound of classical music reached her through the walls. It was soothing and she stroked her body to its rhythm, but whatever she did she couldn't stop remembering images from the night before. Tommy's expressions, how he looked when she surprised him, how genuinely happy he'd been when he'd discovered it was her who had bought his time; how willing, when she challenged or pleasured him beyond even his own expectations. Seeing that light in his eyes and that smile on his face did good things to her. Really good. Heartwarming.

I really like him.

There was no denying it. Whether they were challenging each other sexually, role-playing, or making love, they were entirely attuned. He responded to her wild streak and she couldn't help loving that. Her body craved more of him, and her mind and heart echoed a question over and over—wouldn't it be something to know a man like Tommy Sampson better, to have him be part of your life? But that's not what it had been about. It had been a wild sex game, a chance encounter with a like-minded sexual being. But . . . *if only*, her heart echoed once again. Sighing, she grabbed the quilt, and pulled it over her head.

The door to Clayton's mews cottage was an old world affair with a medieval knocker and a timber-beamed doorway. Tommy lifted the ornate door knocker and rapped. Moments later, Jay appeared in the doorway with a surprised expression on his face.

"Tommy, just the man. You must be psychic."

"Run that by me again." Tommy was confused; he'd been about to explain his presence.

"I was just about to ring you. We need to ask you a favor. Come in, come in." He gestured Tommy into the hallway and pointed in the direction of the sitting room.

"Looks as if we have a coincidence, I need to ask you guys a favor too."

"Coincidence and good timing, in that case." Jay shut the front door and followed him in.

Tommy had visited the place before, and always felt completely oversized in it. The cottage was a highly desirable Tudor residence, but he preferred his warehouse conversion apartment. While here, he always felt he had to keep his elbows in and duck his head in order to avoid bull-in-a-china-shop syndrome, not to mention a concussion.

In the sitting room, Clayton was scrunched on a brown leather sofa with his head in his hands, looking tense. When he heard foot-steps he glanced at the door and his expression broke into a re-lieved smile when he saw who it was.

"Thanks for coming, Tommy."

"No worries," he said, flashing a smile, "but I think there's a misunderstanding here. I called by because I wanted to ask you if you had Kelly's contact details."

Clayton frowned.

"I hadn't called Tommy yet," Jay explained.

"Okay." Clayton shrugged and laughed, sprawling himself more easily into one corner of the sofa, as if the presence of his fa-vorite roadie had brought about a sense of ease.

"What's up?" Tommy looked at Jay for the answer.

"Clayton's considering coming out." Jay paused, his eyebrows lifted, his expression implying the seriousness of the matter.

Tommy tried not to show his surprise, in case that was the wrong thing to do. He lifted his chin in a slow nod. "Right. I see."

"If he goes for it, he'll be giving a press statement tomorrow af-ternoon when he's done at the recording studio. We might need you around, just to keep the paparazzi at bay until we get out of London."

"It's that Kelly woman's fault," Clayton said, shaking his head, one side of his mouth lifted in a sardonic smile.

"Kelly?" This time Tommy couldn't hide his surprise. He thought they were a long way off from the day Clayton was going to come out, unless he was outed by someone who had happened upon the information, like Kelly had, someone with fewer scruples. But apparently Kelly had played a part in this.

Jay indicated Tommy should sit down. "I'll get us some beers."

Clayton's gaze followed Jay as he left the room. "It was the fact that she was hunting you down, she wanted you that much. I believed her when she said she wouldn't use the information about Jay and me. It was because she wanted you that badly that she came after you, the only way she knew how. It really impressed me."

"She said she wanted me?" Tommy couldn't help smiling. Despite her bravado and her oh-so-independent "I'm just doing you back, big boy," approach, she did want him.

Clayton nodded. "Yes, and she said some stuff about me and Jay that made me think . . ." His forehead furrowed again. "I want to be with Jay. If our relationship comes out, it's better if it comes from me. Any other way, and there is going to be a much less positive slant."

"Good point, better to be in control of the information. If you're sure it's the right time for you?" He'd known Clayton for a while, at least three years before he got involved with Jay.

Clayton shrugged. "We're about to go away. We'd only have to suffer the heat for a day or so." He leaned forward, resting his elbows on his knees. "I only need to spend one more day in the studio. We'll do the press release to coincide with the end of that, then do a limited number of appearances before we leave on Tuesday afternoon."

"Makes sense."

Clayton gave him a hopeful smile. "I'd be really grateful if you could be around for this."

"Grateful enough to let me have Kelly's contact details?"

"What is it with you two? You shag, you say good-bye, and *then* you realize you haven't got each other's phone number?"

It sounded crazy, when put that way, and Tommy couldn't help feeling a bit embarrassed. "Um, yeah, kind of. So, have I got a deal?"

Clayton's smile widened. "No can do, I'm afraid. She never gave us any contacts. A bonus fee is all I can offer. Besides, I thought you'd have that information pinned down for yourself by now, Tommy boy."

"Hey, you're doing wonders for my ego."

Clayton laughed. "Sorry, mate. So, what gives? Is she playing hard to get?" He looked every bit the rock god again, and so much more at ease discussing someone else's love life.

Jay appeared with three frosted bottles of beer.

Tommy took one from his hand. "Cheers. Actually, no. I think she's calling my bluff. I told her I wanted to see her again, but she did a disappearing act on me, presumably because I didn't give her my contact details the week before."

"Ah." Jay said, apparently loving the unfolding saga. "She's laid down the gauntlet." He tipped his bottle in Tommy's direction.

"Well, *she* did manage to track *me* down. It's a matter of necessity to match that, and—of course—return the favor." He intended to return each and every favor that she had bestowed on him the night before, in spades.

Clayton laughed and shook his head. "So you two are like . . . playing tag, or kiss chase, or what?"

Tommy shrugged it off with a smile. It was so true, although their game was a whole lot more adult than that. "You could say that, but I'm not about to let her go now."

Jay sat down next to Clayton, and they looked right together. At first, when they told him they were involved, Tommy had felt awkward. He'd never hung out with anyone who was gay before. Very soon after, he'd accepted it easily, because they were so good together. Gender didn't enter into it for him anymore. They were just two people who were meant to be together. Maybe Clayton had always been destined to be with a man, but Jay was obviously the right one.

Even with the decision about coming out weighing heavily on him, Tommy noticed how much happier Clayton was. Jay had been good for him. Before Jay came along, Clayton had been a miserable sod, seldom happy outside of when he was performing or recording. Jay had changed all that, and even though he'd brought about a new set of worries, it was still a positive change.

"So, what's your plan?" Jay was fascinated.

"She left a couple of clues. However long it takes, I'll find her."

"Good man, Tommy boy," Clayton said. "Keep us informed of your progress."

Tommy drained his beer. "I will. And just let me know what time you want me around tomorrow. I'll be there."

As he walked back toward the Tube station, it struck him that even though Kelly was fiercely independent, she impacted people's lives in a unique way. It was her forthrightness, her strength, and determination. She'd come into contact with Clayton and Jay, and it looked as if she had changed them forever.

Me too, most likely.

He liked this strange mixture of qualities she had—the woman who would stop at nothing to get an autograph for her injured friend, the woman who spoke her mind to a leading public figure and made him rethink his life, the woman who fought tooth and nail to be independent, but still had a soft underside that she couldn't always hide. That's the sort of woman Tommy wanted to know better.

Shame she is so bloody prickly, he thought wryly.

The only way to deal with her was on her terms. Capture her; challenge her. He could do that. If something was worth having, it was worth working for. That had been his whole life policy, whether it be following a band he loved around Europe or building a business for the family, hard work was part of the deal. If that's what it was going to take, he was ready. She was worth it.

But first of all, he had to track her down.

ChapterEight

By Tuesday afternoon Kelly was thoroughly annoyed with herself. Even though she tried to concentrate on her job, it was nagging away at her; she could no longer deny her mistake. She shouldn't have walked out on Tommy. That's what she set out to do, to show him how it felt, and her stubborn streak hadn't let her change her mind, even when she had desperately wanted to. Ever since that day she was filled with regret.

Now she had to face up to it, she'd thrown away the chance for something good to prove a point. How stupid was that? She sighed heavily and continued with her vigorous polishing of the free-weights stand.

"You'll polish it away to nothing." Helen looked across the small weights room at her, eyebrows raised questioningly, as she moved from wiping down the stretch bars on the wall to checking the machine settings. "I thought you said you'd burned it all off?"

Kelly frowned, but didn't stop polishing. Overenergetic housekeeping might be a sign of sexual frustration, but she wasn't about to admit it. "I'm just wondering if I am too stubborn for my own good. I got my revenge on Tommy, but it wasn't as sweet as I'd expected."

"You like the man, that's why. It does happen, even to women like you." Helen's smile was teasing.

"Yes, I did like him."

"And did you ever find out if he had a reason for bailing on you that first time?"

"Yes, he had a reason, but I still had to follow my plan through." She put her hands up, rolling her eyes. "Go ahead, laugh at me. I deserve it." She threw her polishing cloth aside in disgust. She did deserve it. She'd messed up.

Helen walked over, put an arm around her shoulders and hugged her. "Stop giving yourself such a hard time. Look, we're done in here. Why don't you take your break now, while it's quiet? Just flip the sign over as you go out and I'll put the cleaning gear away."

"Thanks," Kelly said, returning the hug and heading for the door, not trusting herself to say anything else in case she embarrassed herself. At the door, she flipped the "Closed for maintenance, please use main gym" sign around to read "Gym Open."

She walked along the corridor and up the stairs to the staff room on autopilot, barely noticing anything about her surroundings. After the emotional high of Saturday night with Tommy and her comedown on Sunday, she hit rock bottom on Monday. There was an extreme sense of loss eating away at her. They'd had such fun. *Stop beating yourself up and face it, it's over.*

In the sanctuary of the staff room she went to the refrigerator and pulled out a carton of orange juice, pouring out a glass. Dropping into one of the easy chairs she set the glass on the table next to the various magazines and newspapers that accumulated there. Ruffling her hands through her hair, she stared down at the papers with unseeing eyes, until a headline finally caught her attention. She moved her glass out of the way and stared at the newspaper in complete amazement. ROCK STAR CLAYTON WARREN SINGS NEW TUNE: "I'M GAY AND I'M IN LOVE."

The accompanying picture of Clayton and Jay grinning at the camera took up half the front page of the tabloid. Clayton looked stunning, the happiest she'd ever seen him, his arm around Jay's shoulder as he waved at the camera. She snatched it up and read the photo caption: *Sorry ladies, it looks like hottie Clayton Warren bats for the other team.*

"Well what do you know?" she said, with a soft laugh, her chest suddenly tight and full, her spirits lifting as she read the column.

Clayton Warren, popular music star and lust object of women across the world, spoke briefly to us late last night, following a shocking press statement put out by his new PR representative. Clayton talked about coming out as a gay man and his love for Jay Leonard, pictured here with Clayton outside the Celtic, Clayton's favorite London recording studio, where he's laying down new tracks for the next album.

The two lovers have been involved in a secret affair for seven months. Clayton decided to go public prior to jetting off with Jay for a secluded holiday in the tropics. "I've never been happier," Clayton announced. "Now it's time to tell the world how I feel."

Clayton also revealed that "Squandered," his biggest selling single, was a song he wrote for Jay. "Meeting Jay changed me and my view of everything I'd done up until that point. My emotions were so strong that I felt like I'd squandered my life up until then."

Kelly blinked and paused, remembering how they'd been back-stage, after he'd sung the song as his final encore. Now it made sense. She read on.

Jay Leonard, a music producer who has worked with Clayton for the past year and produced all of his recent material, added, "We hope that Clayton's fans will understand and support him."

When asked if he thought this announcement would affect his career, Clayton said: "I've always been about the music. I will continue to be the musician and performer that people have enjoyed up until now, but—this is about me. When you want to be with someone this badly you've just got to go after it."

Kelly nodded, smiling. "Too right, Clayton. You just have to go after it." She'd done that, she'd gone after Tommy, but it hadn't done her much good.

She looked again at the photo. In the background, she could see another figure, cropped in at the edge of the shot. Her heart fluttered in her chest. Tall and built, she recognized him just from the posture of that magnificent body of his. *Tommy.*

He'd been there. *Of course he'd been there*, she thought. He was that sort of person, loyal, reliable. He was standing by his friend and employer. She lowered the paper with a deep sigh. Reluctantly, she admitted it to herself; she really liked the man. A lot. She'd meant to burn off her attraction with another night of crazy sex, but it only made her hanker after him more. Now it felt like some sort of addiction she couldn't shake.

She knocked back her juice, put the paper down, and stretched, trying to push Tommy out of her mind. But her gaze kept being drawn back to the paper, to Clayton and Jay's smiling faces, and that familiar figure in the background.

"Feeling better?" Helen had stuck her head around the door.

Kelly looked over and forced a nod.

"Good. You've got a session in two minutes."

Kelly held up the newspaper as she stood up. "Have you seen this?"

Helen walked in and, as she closed in on the paper her jaw dropped. "Well, who'd have guessed that?" Taking the paper from Kelly's hand, she scanned the article.

"Are you heartbroken?" Kelly asked, as she retied her sports shoes and shook out her arms and legs, limbering up for her session. She was curious about how the die-hard fans would react.

Helen lowered the newspaper and rolled her eyes. "Are you kidding?" She pointed at the photo of Jay and Clayton. "I used to have wicked dreams about Clayton performing. Just look at this guy." She jabbed the picture of Jay. "Now I'm going to be having dreams about the pair of them getting it on." She fanned herself, laughing. "Two hot blokes. Now that I'd like to see."

Kelly grinned, her mind going back to the image of Jay and

Clayton backstage. "Yes, I bet that would be quite a sight." A soft laugh escaped her.

Helen looked suspicious. "You knew, didn't you?"

Kelly shrugged it off.

"No, you did." Helen pointed at her accusingly, eyes narrowed. "There was something odd about when you went backstage, like part of the story was missing. It wasn't just to do with Tommy, was it?"

There didn't seem to be any reason not to spill, now. "Okay, seeing as it's in the news, I may as well admit it. I accidentally saw Clayton and his lover together."

Helen's eyebrows shot up, her eyes rounding. "Oh, my god, you lucky woman."

Kelly nodded. "Not something I'll forget in a hurry." She winked. Glancing at the clock, she ruffled her hair. "Who's my client?"

Helen folded the paper and tucked it under her arm. "Some bloke who looks like he needs a personal trainer like he needs a hole in the head."

Kelly grimaced. "Not another one looking for girly attention?" It happened from time to time—men who paid for that one-on-one workout when they had no need for it. Mostly they wanted to show off in front of a woman and chat, maybe score.

"Don't worry, this one is easy on the eye. Go, do your duty, soldier." She pointed at the door.

Kelly saluted and headed off. Walking along the corridor, she made a mental note to update the championship league chart and the monthly challenge posters. Hearing the news about Clayton and Jay had lifted her sprits. She was glad. It was good to know that they were happy.

At the door to the small weights room she stopped in her tracks.

The "Closed for maintenance" sign was back on the door. "Huh? I'm sure I changed that."

Peering through the glass door, she couldn't see anyone waiting. The client must be getting changed, she figured, or maybe he thought the gym was really closed. As she walked in she was about to flip the sign, when she sensed another presence. The door shut behind her. Turning, she caught sight of a tall, familiar figure standing behind the door. *Tommy*.

A hot thrill ran through her entire body. Her heart immediately started to race, her hand going to her throat. It was him. He'd found her; he'd been waiting for her.

He kept his hand on the door, holding it shut, and scrutinized her from top to toe. "Ready for a stiff workout, Kelly?"

Oh, yes. "Maybe," she breathed.

His mouth moved in a slow, suggestive smile. "I've been having these relentless dreams about you straddling me, while you spot my weights . . . so, I bought your time for two hours, and then I paid the other customers to get the hell out of here." He stepped closer to her. "You were a hard woman to track down."

She tried to get the image of straddling him out of her mind and lifted her chin, looking him in the eye. "But you managed the job. I'm impressed."

"I never let a client down, and I was still on paid time through Sunday."

"Cheeky."

He nodded. "Ah, but I'm learning from the mistress of cheek."

He looked good in black shorts and a tight white T-shirt, his magnificent body shown to perfection. "How did you find me?"

"You mentioned two consecutive years winning the Southern

Counties canoeing title, that nailed it for me, *Ms. Burton.* I went through the records. Only one woman fitted the bill. Once I'd found out your last name, I started calling round all the gyms in London." He ran a finger down one side of her jaw, softly caressing her chin with his thumb.

"I bought your time. Finding your maintenance sign was an added bonus. Now I've got you all to myself, and it's payback time." His intentions were perfectly clear.

Kelly shook her head, unease rising. If they made love again, she might not be able to walk away from him like she had before.

"And this time you won't get away so easy."

His words only confirmed all her fears. "I shouldn't be doing this on work time." She was reaching out for excuses, denying him, denying herself.

He smiled. "I've figured you out Kelly. You're a strong, independent woman, you take what you want, but you shun emotional involvement."

"So you think you know me now?" Backing away, she could barely take it in. He'd really thought about it.

"You're also honest and true, and you have a strange effect on people. Clayton and Jay came out because of you."

"No." She shook her head. "I saw it in the paper, but it had nothing to do with me."

"You had an impact on them, you made Clayton think. He told me that himself, so don't you go shaking your head at me, madam. I've just seen them off at the airport. Clayton sends his thanks. They both do."

Could it be true? She didn't realize that what she'd said would have any impact on him, other than explaining her own honest intentions. "I just . . . said what I thought."

"That's it exactly. There's something about you. You changed my life too, just by being in it. You're a reckless, headstrong woman, and I love that about you."

Love. Panic hit her. She'd been glad to see him, thrilled, but nerves had taken over. He was talking about stuff that unsettled her.

He continued, ignoring her denial, but standing between her and the door. "Now that you've had your revenge, I wondered if you felt any differently?" His expression looked suddenly serious. "Do you think two hours of your time will be long enough?"

"Long enough for what, exactly?"

"Long enough to talk you into seeing me under regular circumstances." He moved closer, and put his hands on her shoulders, squeezing them. Then he ran his fingers down her back, hauling her body against his.

She could feel him so well, the angles and planes of his body, his strength and muscle, the hard bulge at his groin. Her hands were up and locked against his chest, just like that first night backstage. She couldn't have moved if she wanted to. That alone made her melt. *I need this; I need this man who holds me so tightly.* She shook her head, her hands fisting between them. She was programmed to deny this. "I can't."

"You can."

He made it sound so easy. *Was it easy?*

"All this buying each other's time and tracking each other down could be much better spent with some quality one-on-one time, don't you think?" His expression was watchful, and then he shifted, stroking her shoulders. "But . . . if you insist on playing these kiss-chase games across London, I warn you, I'll give as good as I get."

"Kiss chase?" Why did that make her feel silly?

"That's what Clayton said about us." Humor warmed his expression.

"I guess he has a point." She could feel her cheeks heating, but the idea tickled her. "But, if I run away—"

His eyes darkened. "I'd chase after you." He cursed under his breath, his body taut against hers.

"What if I tied you up again and ran away?"

"You don't want that, you can't."

The response in his eyes made her heart leap. His expression was so serious, the atmosphere between them shifting again.

No, she didn't want that. Could she admit it? She turned her face away.

"Say you'll give it a go," he urged. "Kelly, please. I've let you do things to me that no one else ever has or will. I wouldn't let anyone else."

"You enjoyed it," she murmured, glancing back.

"I did, but because *you* did it to me. . . . I want you badly. You've gotten under my skin; you're in my blood. I think of you all night long when you're not there." He moved against her, gently reminding her of his erection.

Her heart beat hard, as if responding to him no matter what her head told her about independence and being strong. *Give it a try, it might just work.* Yearning was rising up inside her. It was sexual need, yes, but something else too, something much more unusual. "I don't do relationships," she murmured.

"Why are you so dammed prickly? Did someone break your heart?"

"No, I . . ." She'd answered on reflex, but stopped. Her heart thundered in her chest, memories flooding her mind, memories that she'd locked away until now, until Tommy had forced her to see them again. Her dad, packing cases, leaving them. Her mother, heartbroken. *And me, too.* Staring up at him, she realized that he was right. She had been heartbroken; she'd been heartbroken right alongside her mother.

That doesn't mean it won't happen again, fool.

"Are you sure? You don't look sure."

She swallowed it down, barely able to respond. "Okay, maybe you're right."

His eyes searched hers. "Don't expect everyone to be like that person, whoever he was."

Yes, she was meeting the devil halfway, expecting failure before giving life a chance, in the name of self-protection.

He stroked her hair, tentatively drawing her attention back to him. "Will you tell me about it?"

"Maybe. Not now though."

"I understand."

He did, she could see it in him. The big, strong watchful man— so gentle and caring under it all. He'd been the one who had protected Clayton, and now he was here, offering to be with her too. She unfisted her hands, splayed her fingers against his chest. "I'm glad you came after me, but I'm scared."

"I know that. We could take it slowly, see how it goes."

"I'm scared I'll fall for you, that I'll need you."

He lifted an eyebrow. "Would that be so bad?"

"I can't afford to need anyone."

"I think it's too late, Kelly. At least . . . it is for me." He kissed her gently, a mere brush of his lips over hers. The tender touch made her tremble. "I need you, and I think you need me too." His breath was warm on her face. "You came after me. Revenge wasn't the only reason, admit it."

She swallowed. "Maybe you're right." That was hard, but she'd gotten it out.

He stared at her for an age, his eyes searching hers, his mouth moving into a smile.

Please don't push me for more, not yet, she prayed. *I love you, but I'm not ready to say it.*

"Maybe I'm right, huh?"

She nodded, mustering up a warning glance.

"Good, because I don't intend to let you get away." His expression grew mischievous.

They were playing again. Her heartbeat went out of whack, a mixture of relief and desire. She felt steadier. She wanted to challenge him, sexually. "How could you stop me, if I wanted to run?"

She wanted to hear what he would say, needed to know. *Yes. Need.* Damn him, he was making her fall for him by pushing her—pushing her *just* enough.

He didn't reply, but gave her a knowing, suggestive smile, then released her and walked over to the bench press. Reaching behind it, he lifted up a bag, which he placed on the bench. Then he went back to the door, and pulled the blind down, turned the key in the door and gave her a once-over that indicated he meant business. He was pacing himself, building up her anticipation.

She glanced over at the closed-circuit camera and noticed for the first time that there was a towel hanging over it. "You planned this all along."

"I came here with certain intentions, you know that, but the surroundings lent themselves perfectly to my plan." He gestured around the room. "And like you said to me on Saturday, I intend to enjoy it while I'm here."

Suddenly, the exercise equipment looked perfect for a workout of an entirely different kind. A thrill ran through her veins. Tommy flexed his body as if he were getting ready for a real workout. He looked dangerous and, in a room like this, the possibilities for kinky sex were numerous.

"You're all mine, and I'll do anything I have to, to keep you." He went over to the weights bench. Reaching inside the bag, he pulled some lengths of black tape.

She recognized it immediately. It was the same bondage tape she had used on him. "I thought we were done with revenge?"

Heat coursed through her. Instinctively she took a step back, but she wanted to be chased, to be hunted by this man who responded to her needs so well.

He ran the lengths of black PVC tape through his hands, the look in his eyes dangerously arousing. "You're going to be mine, and you will have to take everything I give you."

"I'll only get my revenge next time."

"Next time?" He smiled insinuatingly, and wound the length of tape around his fists, stretching it tight. "If it's anything like last time, you'll drive me insane."

"That could be entertaining," she retorted, her blood rushing with excitement. Her heart pounded against the wall of her chest.

She noticed his gaze drifting over her breasts as they rose and fell inside her tight Lycra top.

He moved up against her in a flash.

Her hands clasped around his head, scrunching into his hair, reveling in that sensation she'd longed to feel again. Stroking him beneath his ear, where she knew his hidden erogenous spot was, she bit her lip and chuckled.

"There's no need for that." He squeezed her closer; let her feel how hard he was.

She hummed approvingly, her body soaring. "The chase has been kind of fun."

"The capture will be even better, I assure you." He put one large hand around the base of her neck, resting the palm on her collarbone, and walked her back toward the wall.

Overwhelmed, she moved under his control. She felt the stretch bars against her back and exclaimed.

"You are the most beautiful, crazy woman I've ever known." His hands moved to her wrists and he lifted her arms over her head, to the bar above.

She didn't fight him.

Once he had tied her wrists to the metal bar, he gave her jaw a gentle bite, making her smile inside. He tested the range of movement in her wrists. "Can you move your hands?"

"I didn't think you wanted me to move."

"I want you to be able to struggle, just a little bit. It's more fun that way."

Heat rose to the surface of her skin. Instinctively, her hands gripped at the rail, testing it out.

He nodded approvingly. He ran his hands over her prone torso, enflaming her breasts. "The need to be inside you has been a more powerful force than anything I've ever known. The moment I saw you outside the door, my dick got hard."

She snaked within his grasp, her body flushed with heat, his raw words sending flare after flare of red-hot lust through her. Her crotch was damp. She wanted to feel him there, longed for it.

He put his fingers inside the waistband of her gym pants, breathing along the skin of her collarbone, before slowly dropping down to squat in front of her, taking her pants and underwear down with him. He looked up at her, his gaze making a slow passage over her body. "I'm dying to taste you. If you promise to sit on my face again, I'll be your slave forever."

He looked so strong, so mighty, and when he knelt there looking up at her that way, saying those words, something came undone inside her. "Tommy, please," she murmured, her breath catching in her throat.

He reached up, opening up her thighs, his fingers plunging into her sex, testing her. "So wet," he murmured, and then he leaned in, taking her in his mouth, working her fast and hard.

Her clit pounded anxiously when he rolled his tongue back and forth over it, sucking on her as she writhed. Back and forth, the strokes maddening her. Then he did that thing with his teeth, rubbing them over her flesh, grazing the sensitive swell of her clit and suddenly she was coming fast, her womb heavy with release as she moaned and wriggled, fluid running down her thighs.

He stood up, wiped his face with the back of his hand, grinning, and pulled a condom from his pocket. Tearing it open, he reached inside his shorts for his cock, rolling the rubber onto it quickly. He grappled her buttocks into his hands, and then lifted her. "Are you ready for me?"

She nodded, anticipating the feeling of that hard hot shaft that her body craved so much.

He smiled, but he didn't enter her. Stepping back, he lurched her body away from the wall.

"Oh god." She flashed him a glance and laughed, her hands riding around the bar, tightening on it. So this is why he had tested her range of movement. He was challenging her, challenging her to keep hold while he rode her.

He wrenched her thighs apart, and stood between them. "Strong enough to take it?"

The mere thought of him there, his powerful male body thrusting into her while she held on for dear life, totally at his mercy, just about made her come on the spot. But the challenge he gave flared through her. She grasped the bars tighter, tensing her body. "Give me your best shot, big man."

He nodded; his eyes filled with dark promise. Shoving one strong arm under her buttocks to support her, the other hand directed his cock toward her entrance. "I want to possess you in every way possible. I want you bound and blindfolded. I want you to suffer with need. I want to feel you struggle against me, I want you to beg me to make you come . . . and make you wait."

She cried out, holding on tight, her body stretched out, taut and wired.

The head of his cock was just inside, but he was holding back. Resting easily between her thighs, he had her strung out, physically and emotionally. "I know you're strong enough to match me."

His words bit into her, making her grip the rail and pull, rising up in front of him. "Tommy Sampson," she breathed, staring at him accusingly, and with as much savvy as she could muster, "you are one kinky bloke."

"Just as well I found you then, isn't it, kinky lady?" He pushed his cock deeper.

She clutched at it, her body melting onto it, relief hitting her. He had found her, and she was glad.

The muscles in his neck tightened. He was still holding back. "Together we can be happy just trying to out-kink each other."

"Sounds good to me," she about managed to reply, heat breaking out all over her body. The back of her neck was damp, the undersides of her breasts inside her Lycra top growing clammy.

"Do I have that in writing?" He withdrew his cock, moving it outside her entrance again, pressing against her with the hard head but not pushing in. He was teasing her to the max.

She clenched with loss, but she had no control over her lower body, it was entirely in his hands. "No need. I might not give it often, but my word is good, you know that." She braced her arms, lifted up against the bars again and looked him in the eyes. "I want you, Tommy."

"Good, because you've got me." He rode her deep, ramming up against her cervix.

She cried out, her hungry eyes devouring him.

As he moved, thrusting hard, his brow was drawn down in concentration, the muscles in his neck corded. His hands clutched her buttocks tight, squeezing the flesh as he thrust into her. He was as driven as she, his cock seeming to swell again inside her, on every thrust. He was ready to blow.

Her sex was stretched to capacity and felt unfeasibly full. The angle was so good, and his rolling hip thrusts sent her back to the edge of ecstasy, fast.

"It feels so good, right there inside you." He spoke through gritted teeth, and then his mouth opened and his eyes closed. His body bowed back at the shoulders as his hips thrust deep into her.

She cried out, the thrust driving so high and deep, her cervix was palpating, her womb flooded, her chest congested, and her throat on fire.

His cock lurched, jerking inside her.

Her body responded, her sex spasmed and clenched. "Tommy, I'm coming." Her clit burned, a loop of tension uncoiling inside her. She bucked against him, and her arms weakened, her hands feeble and grasping at the rail, her damp palms sliding on the metal surface. "Oh god, I can't hold on."

His eyes flashed, and he moved under her, thrusting her up, so that her weight rested on his hips, his cock angled deep inside her. He jerked his head, flashing his damp hair back from his forehead, and gave a soft, hoarse laugh. "I'm here, I won't let go. I'm right here."

Winded, she shuddered and came again, her sex flooded, her head falling forward onto his shoulder.

He reached up, moving around her, wrenching the bondage tape from the bar.

Panting, she moved and latched her hands around his face, lifting her head up and wrapping her legs around his hips. "Isn't this how we started?"

He smiled, holding her easily, his hands stroking her back. "Things have changed a bit since that night, haven't they?"

132

"Yes, they have. Hold me, Tommy." She was still struggling to catch her breath. Her limbs were weak and shaking, her hands clutching at him.

"Like I said, I'm right here."

She nodded, looking into his eyes. She felt raw inside, her chest aching. The pain of the emotion felt good, though. It made her feel alive, really alive, and for the first time ever, Kelly Burton wanted her heart to ache some more.

Watch Me

SASHA WHITE

Prologue

What is it about the tease that's so hot?

You know what I'm talking about. That tingle you get between your thighs when someone exciting catches your eye, or when *you* catch his. The lingering looks, the hair toss, the silent communication. That time when your blood heats up and your body awakens as you feel the magic of "what if?"

It's almost . . . intoxicating.

I used to flirt a lot. Men used to flirt with me. Then I got married. I haven't gained weight or let myself go, but somehow, I've changed. I know it, and they know it. I think it's because the chase is over. The magic of flirting, the heightened awareness that arcs between two people, the building of anticipation . . . it's gone.

And I don't know exactly when, or how, it disappeared.

The sad thing is, it also seems to have disappeared between my husband and me.

Now, don't get me wrong. I love my husband. Grant is still very attractive in every way, and leaving him has never occurred to me. I'd never cheat on him, either.

Yet, I can't deny that a certain restlessness has been building in me for some time.

Chapter One

The bed shifted beneath me, and my hand stretched out over the cotton, seeking warm flesh. When I found only empty space, my eyes cracked open and I saw Grant's muscular back as he perched on the edge of the bed, running his hands through his thick, dark hair.

Inching closer, I reached out and stroked my hand over those delicious muscles, all the way down to the small of his back. The sigh that broke the early-morning silence as my fingers ran through the fine dusting of hair there was soft.

My body warmed, waking up slowly. With a lazy touch, I walked my hand around his waist, heading for that morning hard-on that could be used to really wake me up and start my Monday off right. But as I reached him, the alarm clock sounded and Grant smacked it.

He flopped back onto the bed and wrapped his arms around me. Soft lips touched my forehead in a loving kiss before he spoke regretfully. "Sorry, babe. I've got a big meeting, and I can't be late."

He gently rubbed his stubbled cheek against my jaw before pressing his mouth to mine. His tongue darted out for a quick swipe across my lips and I parted them, eager to take things further.

With a tortured groan and a sharp pat on my backside, he stood up and went down the hall to the bathroom. I tried not to think about it, tried not to let my body's disappointment invade my brain. Instead, when I heard the shower come on, I rolled over and went back to sleep.

Fresh from the shower and wrapped in a silk kimono-style gown, I strolled into the bedroom with coffee cup in hand. Ugh! Monday mornings were never my favorite. Mornings in general were hell, but Mondays were the worst. Which is why I liked my job at the boutique so much. As manager, I didn't need to be in the store until ten and that gave me the extra time to become human before facing the public.

Only one thing really wakes me up with a smile on my face, and that's morning wake-up sex. I'd tried to get Grant into it that morning, but he hadn't been interested. It sort of felt that way a lot lately. Like I was a little kid trying to get attention from her favorite teacher.

I stepped back from the mirror and studied my reflection— married almost four years and still looking good. I hadn't gained any weight, and I certainly didn't look thirty-four years old, so that wasn't why the spark had gone out of our sex life. And by no spark, I don't mean we don't have sex. We do, it's just not exciting anymore . . . or often enough.

When I was single, two weeks without sex wasn't a big deal. I was used to it. But sleeping next to the sexiest man I knew night after night, and not being touched and teased or set on fire the way I *knew* he could . . . it was hell. A sneak-up-on-you, long, slow-roasting hell.

Out of the corner of my eye, I caught a movement. I spun around and saw a man on the roof of my neighbor's house. Hmm. That's what that nagging pounding was. I'd thought it was just my brain protesting its awakened state.

I couldn't see the roofer's face very well, but even at a distance I could tell he had a killer body. And as usual, the sight of bulging muscles made my pulse kick up a notch.

Shoving the image of the roofer's hard body to the back of my mind, I went to work on my makeup. Ladies weren't supposed to drool over men who weren't their husbands.

Unfortunately, my eyes wouldn't listen to my brain. I kept glancing in the mirror and checking him out. That was when I noticed he was glancing my way too. Adrenaline started to ease into my bloodstream, a long-absent awareness settled in, and a naughty idea sprouted in my half-awake mind.

Exaggerating my primping in the mirror, I piled my russet curls on top of my head and let the belt of my robe work itself loose. I stuck pins into my hair randomly so it had the sexy "just tumbled" look to it, and I bent deeper over the dresser.

The next time he glanced my way, if he was paying attention, he'd see the bottom of my butt cheeks peeking out from below the edge of my robe. After applying my mascara I straightened and flicked a glance at his reflection. He was still working, but slowly. In the ten seconds I watched him, he glanced my way three times.

"Yes!" I hissed under my breath. A tingle of pride, of awareness, whipped through my body.

Then I realized what I was doing and my spirits fell. Flashing a stranger was the sort of thing Ginger would do. She was the "wild one," not me. That's not to say I was an angel, but when it comes to wild-and-crazy things, my tattooed and pierced spirit sister beat me out by a mile.

However, when I saw the roofer pause in his work and look my way again, I spun around quickly so my robe flared out, and gave him a quick glimpse of my naked body. I couldn't stop myself. Pulling a casual sundress from the closet, I tossed it on the bed with a flick of my wrist and went back to the dresser.

A quick glance in the mirror assured me I still had the stranger's attention, and arousal burned low in my belly. With a shrug of my shoulders, the robe fell to the floor and I stood naked. Trying to look natural, I reached into the dresser drawer and pulled out a pair of panties. With slow, teasing movements, I slid them up my legs and adjusted them on my hips, then snatched my dress from the bed. Once the material settled loosely over my curves I gave myself a last critical look in the mirror.

A flush had bloomed on my cheeks and my blue eyes sparkled. Squelching a tinge of discomfort at my behavior, I peeked over my shoulder and saw that my audience was still enthralled. Energized, I picked up my unneeded coffee and strolled from the room, ready to start the week with my long-lost sense of allure back in full force.

Chapter Two

I hate you, Bethany Mack."

"What? Why?" I laughed at the grumpy look on my best friend's face. Ginger Harrison wasn't any more of a morning person than I was. In fact, she was even worse. But she didn't normally greet me when I walked into the store with such a dramatic statement.

"You're smiling. That means you got some this morning. And I, single and horny woman that I am, hate you for it." She turned her back on me and continued to straighten the display of purses and handbags in front of her.

"No, I didn't *get any* this morning. Although I did try." I toyed briefly with the idea of telling her what I'd done, but just shrugged when she raised an eyebrow at me. "And . . . you're only single because you want to be."

I went to the back of the store, dropped off my purse, poured myself a cup of coffee, and went back out on the floor to chat with Ginger.

Rosa's was a small boutique that targeted the businesswomen of Vancouver, as well as the upper-class wives of businessmen. The clothes ranged from casual khakis and knit T-shirts to fancy party dresses worthy of a New Year's Eve ball, all made with the same meticulous quality. It was a quiet shop most of the time, but that didn't bother me because I didn't feel any real passion for fashion. It was just a job to me.

I didn't have a passion for anything else either. Well, except for Grant. I figure that's why I'd gone from part-time clerk while in college, to full-time store manager ten years later.

Ginger was just the opposite of me. She had too many passions to count. Which is why she was still a part-time clerk. She was always taking night classes in some subject or trying out other jobs. When she got stuck for money, or pissed off at some other boss, she came back to Rosa's. She knew I'd always hire her back, and I'd work around any other commitments she had.

I always loved it when Ginger worked on a display. With a good sense of balance and color, she knew how to catch the eye. It wasn't often she took the time to fuss with displays though. Despite the fact that she wasn't what most people termed "classy," what with her pierced nose and the sometimes visible tattoo on her back, she was the best salesgirl in the store, and she rarely had the time, or the inclination, to do anything but sell.

The fact that she was arranging the handbags first thing in the morning, when she'd normally be in the back room, mainlining as much coffee as she could, told me something was on her mind.

"The display looks good." I nodded at the way she had the accessories organized. It was hard to make a rack of handbags look good, but she'd managed to do it.

"Sometimes being single is the best thing in the world," she said, ignoring my compliment. "Other times, I hate the lack of a regular sex life. And what do you mean 'you tried' to get some this morning?"

A couple walked into the store, and we both turned to smile at them. I watched as the woman browsed and the man trailed behind her. "You could have sex anytime you wanted, *if* you really wanted to. All you have to do is smile at a man and he leaves a trail of drool as he chases after you, and you know it."

"Yeah, but unlike you I haven't met one worth keeping. So until then," she said glancing at me, the mischief in her big brown Bambi eyes barely hiding something darker, "I'll keep my independence, and enjoy the occasional bout of wild monkey sex."

I sputtered and tried not to choke on the sip of coffee I'd just taken. "Well, enjoy it while you can, the wild monkey sex doesn't last long once you find Mr. Right."

That was when I noticed the way the man kept looking over his shoulder at me. When our eyes met, I smiled. It was my polite shopkeeper's smile, and I was surprised when he winked at me in return.

"Beth!"

"What?"

"You're flirting." Ginger's full lips stretched into a grin.

Heat crawled up my neck and I pushed away from the shelving unit. "I am not."

"Yes, you are. And don't think I didn't notice the fact that you ignored my question about the lack of sex this morning." She followed me over to the till where I shuffled some papers and tried to look busy. "But I'll let it go, for now, in favor of reminding you that it's okay to flirt. You're married, not dead!"

"And you're single, not dead. So why aren't you the one flirting?"

Her shoulders lifted and fell casually while she looked anywhere but at me. An idea hit. I needed to get out, and I got the feeling Ginger really needed to talk, so I reached across the sales desk and clasped her hand. "Why don't we go for drinks after work? Grant's probably working late again anyway."

"I can't tonight. I have class. What about Thursday?"

I should've known. "What are you taking now?"

"Photography." Her eyes lit up with excitement. "Tonight's the first class."

"I thought you already took photography?"

She nodded. "I did. But this is a class on black-and-white photography. Totally different."

"Okay." I shrugged. "Thursday it is. It'll be fun!"

A grin split Ginger's pretty face. "It will! It's been too long since we went out together."

She slapped her hand on the counter before heading over to the shopping couple with a bounce to her step. Ginger started talking to the woman, and the man turned away from them and smiled at me again. It was a small, secretive smile. As if we shared something.

I'd never seen the guy before, and we didn't share anything. But the heat in his gaze reminded me of my morning watcher, and I couldn't stop myself from licking my lips, and smiling provocatively.

Chapter Three

I was right. Grant did work late that night.

It was after nine o'clock and I was ensconced on the sofa, feeding my secret addiction by watching season two of *Angel* on DVD *again*, when Grant entered the house.

"What a day!" He dropped onto the couch next to me.

"Bad?" I asked.

"Nah, not bad, just hectic. I know taking this promotion was the right thing to do for us, and our future, and I know I can do the job. It's just taking more time getting settled in than I expected." He gave me a tired smile. "I'm beat, babe."

I cupped his jaw and pulled his head down so I could kiss him. The rasp of his stubble tickled the palm of my hand and I lazily stroked his tongue with mine. Before I could deepen the kiss he pulled back.

"I need a shower, then I'm crawling into bed. Will you be long?"

When I shook my head no, he turned and headed up the stairs. I toyed with the idea of joining him, but he'd seemed distracted and doubt that I'd be welcome niggled at me.

My chest tightened and I tried to refocus on the show, but couldn't quite manage. The cynical side of my brain was prompting me to wonder if Grant was having an affair. I mean, our sex life hadn't exactly been rockin' lately, and that would seem to be a reasonable assumption. Except, I knew he wouldn't do that.

With midnight black hair and piercing green eyes, Grant had the look and the attitude of a bad boy, which he had blatantly been when I'd first met him. But like all those rakes and playboys I'd read about in romance novels, when he gave his love, he was fierce and loyal.

And he loved me.

He wasn't cheating on me. He was just preoccupied. His recent promotion from ad designer to account executive at one of Vancouver's top advertising firms had him working almost nonstop. We'd talked about it before he accepted the promotion, and we knew it would be hard. I just don't think either of us knew *how* hard.

The shower turned off with a protesting squeal from the pipes and I tracked his footsteps above me to the bedroom. Before I could think twice, I switched off the TV and dashed up the stairs. When I walked into the bedroom, Grant was stretched out naked on the bed, one arm bent, hand tucked behind his head, eyes closed.

"Yum," I whispered as I climbed onto the bed and slowly straddled his body. "Look what I found sleeping in my bed."

He didn't move, but for a small twitch of his lips. Leaning forward, I tasted that half smile briefly before nibbling my way over to his ear. I nuzzled the soft spot behind his ear and spoke softly. "Such delicious flavor you have."

His chest brushed against mine as it shook with silent laughter. Sitting up, I quickly pulled off the baggy T-shirt I'd donned when I got home from work earlier, leaving me in nothing but my cotton bikini panties. I wiggled myself down his body, letting the tips of my nipples scrape along his torso. After nudging his legs apart a bit I lay down, my body snug on top of his, his stiffening cock nestled nicely between my breasts as I scraped my nails across one male nipple and my teeth across the other.

His fingers weaved into my hair, cupping the back of my head. He didn't try to direct me, or take control. He just let me enjoy myself. I ran my fingers through the crisp curls that covered his muscles, loving the way my fingertips tingled as they followed the trail to his belly button. I slid a bit lower, rimming the hole with the tip of my tongue as his cock bobbed, looking for the warm home of my breasts that had disappeared.

Warmth flowed through me at the feel of my husband's body beneath me, the ripple of his muscles under my fingertips as I skimmed over his torso. One hand dipped down to travel up the inside of his thigh at the same time my tongue and teeth scraped over his hip bone. His lower belly tightened, and his breathing grew ragged as I let my hot breath tease over his hardness.

This was my passion. The rightness that I felt in my soul every time I touched him, every time I gave him pleasure. This is where I belonged.

His fingers tightened in my hair and his hips lifted slightly off the bed. I circled the base of his shaft with my fingers and took him in my mouth. A low moan echoed in the room as my tongue swirled and my lips tightened. I sucked gently, raising and lowering my head, taking him in and out. He heated up, his cock swelling and hardening in my mouth until I could feel him hit the back of my throat.

I kept working him for a couple more minutes, my free hand sneaking between my own legs. My clit was hard and my entrance slick. He hadn't touched me, but he didn't need to. Just knowing I was pleasing him was a turn-on for me.

After rubbing my clit for a couple more seconds I'd had enough. Pleasing Grant *was* a turn-on, but I wanted more. I wanted him deep inside me.

Pulling away, I got rid of my panties and straddled him once more. This time his eyes were open, watching me as I got into position. Gripping him with one hand, I rubbed the head of his cock up and down my slit, and then impaled myself on him.

A gasp escaped my lips and I wiggled, loving the fullness of Grant buried deep inside me. His free hand rested on my thigh as I started rocking. It wasn't long before his fingers tightened on my leg, and my insides clenched in response. Our eyes were locked together even though he remained still with one hand behind his head. His lips parted as his breath came faster, his brow puckered, and his cock throbbed hotly as I rotated and thrust my hips. I was almost there, the heat from within spreading to all my nerve endings. I caught his gaze and ran my hands over my torso, up over my ribs and to cup my own breasts.

It was then that his hand came out from under his head and he gripped both my hips. He grunted as he thrust fast and hard into me, and I pinched my nipples, watching heat flare deep in his eyes and feeling sharp pleasure shoot from the hard tips straight to my core. With one last growl, Grant held me tight to him, his cock twitching and jerking inside me as he came. Without thinking, I reached down and tweaked my clit, sending pleasure sweeping throughout my body to every nerve.

I collapsed on top of him, and he rolled to his side. Warm lips pressed against my forehead as he cuddled me close. "That was hot, babe. Just what I needed," he whispered drowsily. "Thanks."

Then he was asleep.

I lay there for a few minutes, wishing he hadn't fallen right to sleep. Then I got up and turned out the bedroom lights before crawling back into bed. I pulled a blanket from the foot of the bed to cover us and snuggled up close to my husband, trying not to remember how we used to be able to go all night.

How he never used to get enough of me.

By six o'clock Thursday night I was more than ready for a drink. "You have my cell phone if you need me, right?" I pointed a stiff finger at the pretty blond behind the cash register at Rosa's.

Samair had been working for me for a few years, first as a seamstress just doing alterations and such, and then later on as a salesgirl. She had a wonderful way with customers. She'd talk them into trying on items they'd never look twice at, and then employ her sewing expertise to customize them to fit so that even the most self-conscious woman felt like Wonder Woman.

"I have your cell number, and I know where you're going to be. It'll be all right, I have closed the shop for you before, you know?" Her angelic blue eyes twinkled as she shooed me out the door.

"I know, but Rosa called earlier today and that usually precedes her dropping by."

Samair propped her hands on her plump hips and flashed me a polished smile. "If Rosa drops by, I'll introduce myself. I've worked here for more than two years; it would be nice to meet the owner sometime. Now go! Ginger is waiting."

My cell phone sang out to me less than a minute after I walked out of the boutique. With a quick glance at the caller ID, I flipped the phone open. "I'll be there in ten minutes, Ginger."

I exited the shopping mall and immediately felt the blast of our late-summer heat wave. Thank God the mall was air-conditioned, or work would be pure hell. It was clear that someone forgot to mention to Mother Nature that September was not supposed to be the hottest month of the year.

"Hurry up. There's a few hunks in here that might steal me away if you take any longer than that." The words were meant to be lighthearted, but there was a note in Ginger's voice that was almost sad. Almost resigned.

Nine minutes later I strode into the air-conditioned pub and spotted Ginger right away. Seated at the bar with a man on each side, she looked like she was having a great time. My plan of dashing to the ladies' room to freshen my lipstick and fluff my hair died a quick death when she saw me in the mirror behind the bar and waved me over.

She jumped off the bar stool and winked at the bartender.

"We're going to go sit on the patio, Darren. Will you send out a jug of sangria for us?"

The blond nodded, a look of pure adulation on his face. The two men who had flanked her groaned in protest, but Ginger shot them a look and said, "Maybe if you boys behave, we'll invite you to join us after we have some girl talk."

She grabbed my arm and pulled me back out in the sunshine. We found a table where she could sit in the sun, and I had shade from the big umbrella. Perfect for us both.

"You sure you want to abandon your admirers at the bar?"

"Please." Ginger slipped dark sunglasses over her eyes and waved a hand airily. "They're just looking to get laid, and I'm not interested."

I swallowed a sigh. The men who were "just looking to get laid" hadn't even glanced at me. I was back to being invisible to the opposite sex. Even Grant hadn't done more than cuddle up and kiss me softly before falling asleep the last couple of nights.

The bartender delivered a pitcher of the fruit-enhanced wine with two glasses, and we sat back in our chairs, each of us with our own thoughts until Ginger broke the silence.

"I'm sick of men."

That gave me pause.

Men drool over Ginger whenever she smiles at them for more than one reason. With her chestnut hair cut in a short pixie style that framed her delicate features, she was gorgeous. The small diamond stud in her left nostril, the colored hair gel she occasionally used, and the tattoo that played peek-a-boo from the waistband of her jeans only enhanced her looks. More than that, her exuberant sexuality was obvious in the way she walked and the tilt to her smile. No way was she really giving up on men.

Unless . . . "Does that mean you're thinking of trying out women?"

She wiggled back in her seat and faced me. "Well, I've been trying the celibate thing, but it doesn't work so well for me. So yeah, the thought crossed my mind."

ChapterFour

I sipped my drink, concentrated on the citrus-flavor burst that came with it, and contemplated how to respond.

Ginger let out a husky chuckle. "Don't worry, Beth. I'm not going to hit on you."

"I'm not worried. I couldn't care less if you preferred women over men, you should know that." Although, for a split second, I *was* hurt that even she wasn't hitting on me. With a shake of my head I leaned forward in my seat. "But I do admit that I'm shocked about the celibacy thing. What's bugging you, sweetie?"

The endearment slipped out, as it often did when I spoke to Ginger. She was only two years younger than me, but for some reason, I often felt like the big sister.

"Nothing's *bugging* me really. I'm just tired of the games, the effort it takes to find a boyfriend."

"That you're even looking for a relationship is news to me. You're always going on about how you love being single. You love living alone, you love your space and not having to tell anyone what you're doing or where you are. A steady man would change that."

"I know." She nodded slowly then sighed. "But sometimes I wonder what it would be like to have someone to curl up on the couch with and watch TV. Or to wake up to."

"Sometimes?"

"More than sometimes." Her shoulders drooped a little and I realized she was serious. She really wasn't happy.

"Oh, honey. You've always been so happy on your own. What's changed?"

"Nothing's changed," she said. "That's the problem. Men still chase me, but as soon as I let one catch me, it's over. I start thinking that a relationship might not be a bad thing, and they're heading for the door."

"Some men just aren't the relationship type, Ginger."

A movement out of the corner of my eye caught my attention, and I glanced over Ginger's shoulder just before the bartender reached our table. He set a basket of chips and salsa in the middle of the table and grinned at Ginger.

"I'm off work at nine. What do you say we get together?"

Her eyebrows raised from behind her sunglasses as if to say "See what I mean?"

I covered my snicker by taking another drink.

"Not tonight, sugar." Ginger flashed a sultry smile and trailed her fingertip over the hand I had on the table. "I already have plans."

Darren's face fell, but only for a second. "I'm here five nights a week, pretty lady. So, you know where I am next time you need some company."

My giggles escaped when he was only five feet away. "Someone needs to tell that boy that it takes more than a basket of free chips and dip to make an impression."

"That's just it, Beth. He didn't want to make an impression. He just wanted to get laid."

"You can't know that."

"Sure I can. If he'd wanted anything more than sex, he'd have asked for my phone number or said something about having dinner together when he got off work. Anything more than 'Let's get together, babe.'" Her voice deepened until she sounded like some cheesy macho man.

Good point. "Okay, so he's a bartender looking for a good time. Not all men are like that."

"But those seem to be the only men interested in me, Beth. I've *never* had a man want to stick around for more than a good time." Her expression turned angry for a split second before it settled into one of stubborn woe. "I think it's me, not them."

Sympathy welled up in my chest. I remembered what it was like to feel lonely. To wonder if I'd ever find someone to love, someone that would love me back. "It's not you, Ginger. It's just not the right time for you. Have you met someone you want to have a real relationship with?"

"No one in particular. I mean, there was John a while back. He was a great lover, and he treated me real nice. He stocked my favorite root beer in the fridge, and we actually had a few dates that didn't end up with us in bed. But, as soon as I started to think there could be more than sex between us, he decided he wanted to give his marriage another chance."

I knew all about the guy she'd met online. He'd told her he was separated from his wife, and she believed him because he lived in a small apartment with little furniture and no signs of female habitation. I think he was either single, and wanted to stay that way, or still married, and the apartment was his secret love-nest type of place. He'd never spent the night with her, or let her stay the whole night with him. To me, that raised red flags.

But, I also knew that when they were together he'd treated her better than most men in her past had. And she'd fallen for him.

"I know you liked John, but he wasn't good enough for you."

Her smile was a little sad. "I know you think that, Bethany. The thing is, he's the only one I've met that's treated me like more than a fuck, even if that's all I really was."

"Did you ever think that men treat you that way because you let them?"

I couldn't see her eyes, hidden behind her sunglasses, but the corners of her mouth tightened and I knew she hadn't liked my comment. "You might be starting to desire a real relationship, but that's new for you. And the attitude you show men hasn't changed, even if your wants have. And as long as you keep acting like the party girl around them, they'll keep treating you like one."

She took off her sunglasses and leaned in. Her eyes were bright with hurt and anger when she spoke. "So you honestly think that if I stop going out and having a good time that Mr. Right will show up on my doorstep?"

"No," I said firmly. "I think going out and having fun is okay.

Flirting is great, but I think that you need to value yourself more in order for them to value you."

"What's that supposed to mean?"

"As archaic as it is . . . it means stop sleeping with a guy on the first date."

Ginger flopped back into her chair. "Shit."

I tried not to laugh. I did. But a giggle escaped at the mutinous look on her face.

"It's not fair! Just because I'm not afraid to admit I love sex doesn't mean it's all I have to offer."

"I know, sweetie." I patted her shoulder, and then refilled our glasses while she pouted. "But it's true, attitude is everything. When you walk, talk, and flirt like you're on the prowl, men react to that. When you act like all you have to offer is sex, all you're going to get is men who want sex. It'll happen, Ginger. Mr. Right will stroll into your life when you least expect it."

ChapterFive

For the next week, the heat was unbearable. Grant worked a lot, and although I saw him every morning and every night, I was starting to feel lonely, even a little lost. And I hated it.

Everything in my life was going according to plan, only I wasn't enjoying it anymore. I'd partied and enjoyed my twenties, fallen in love just before my thirtieth birthday, and married Grant before I was thirty-one. He got a promotion and we were both working toward a secure future. A baby was the next logical step, but Grant and I both agreed we weren't ready for that step yet. In the meantime, though, I couldn't help feeling like we were treading water.

We were in a rut, and I was bored.

When I'd headed out for work that morning, it was only to discover that the heat wave had finally killed my sick car.

"I'll pick up a new radiator hose on my way home from work tonight, and it'll be running again for you tomorrow," Grant had promised when I'd called him at work.

It was great to have a husband that knew a thing or five about cars. But, it also meant he'd be busy in the garage that night, *and* that I was stuck with the bus for transportation. At least it was only for one day.

The smart thing to do would be to talk to Grant about how I felt. Especially now that I'd finally figured it out. We'd always been able to talk about everything and anything in the past, but I didn't want to be the whiny, needy wife who nagged him when he was working so hard.

I'd fallen in love with Grant on our first date, before we'd even left the pub. His cocky attitude and unshakable confidence, not to mention the sizzling good-night kiss that first night, had been hard to resist. His devilish playfulness had been just what I needed.

We still talked and joked, and cuddled and laughed together. But so often Grant was too tired to do more than watch TV or fall straight into bed at night. We didn't spend enough time together, and we certainly weren't making love often enough.

Sex was a growing issue, in my mind. It seems the scientists were right when they said women hit their sexual peak in their thirties, because I was in a state of constant craving. A sundress with no panties had become my regular uniform. Not just because of the summer heat, but because I'd become a masturbating maniac.

While I was waiting for the bus I discovered that if I swayed on my feet slightly, shifting my weight back and forth, the movement caused the skirt of my sundress to swing. And *that* created the tiniest of breezes on my privates. One that alternately made me cooler, and hotter.

A bead of sweat ran down the side of my face. Another followed it, then another turning it into a steady stream. Waiting for the bus in the evening twilight wasn't any cooler than it had been that morning. Puddles of sweat were forming between my breasts, between my thighs, behind my knees, and where my hair lay heavily on the back of my neck. It had been a humid day in the city and nightfall had just made the air thicker. Everyone I saw looked wilted around the edges.

It was then that I realized I was getting admiring looks from some of the male passersby. My little speech to Ginger about attitude popped into my head, and I felt like I'd been hit by lightning. It applied to me too! I was feeling sexy because of the no panties thing, and it must've shown.

The bus pulled up to the curb, and as the doors opened for me, I heard a raucous voice call out "Hey, baby, no need for the bus, I'll give you a *real* ride!"

Without looking to see who it was I climbed into the bus and moved to the back with a grin on my face. It didn't matter who had said it, or that some women might've been offended by the comment. I wasn't. It felt great to have a man see me as so attractive and sexy that he'd had to call out, stranger or no.

I was the only pickup at that stop so the bus started moving before I reached my seat and an invigorating breeze brushed over my body from the open windows. Dropping down onto the bench seat, I smiled at the rumpled-looking businessman across from me before leaning my head back against the window and letting the air rushing in from the window sweep over me.

The bus stopped a couple more times, but no one else moved to the back of the bus. So when it pulled onto the freeway, the man in the suit and I were alone, and directly across from each other.

The wind from the window felt amazing so I pulled the top of my dress away from my chest and let the breeze flow over my exposed skin. A shiver ran down my spine and my nipples hardened from the shock. Sensing another kind of heat on my skin, I peeked out from under my eyelashes to see that the man across from me had his eyes glued to my chest, as if in a trance.

Lifting my head away from the window, I glanced down. The material of my dress was once again plastered to my small breasts and my nipples were poking rudely against the fabric, but everything was covered up so I didn't know what he was fixated on.

When I looked back at him, he was reading the paper once again. Resuming my relaxed pose I watched him from under my eyelashes. He was an okay-looking guy. A bit too young for my taste, even though he wore a suit. Not that it mattered. I was married, but . . . I wasn't dead. Every few seconds, he would glance over at me, his eyes running hungrily over my body.

The little devil that had reared its head last week with the roofer tapped me on the shoulder once again. *It's all about attitude*, I reminded myself.

I brought my hand up and pushed my hair lazily off my face, letting my fingers trail softly to my neck, then wiped at the beads of sweat there. As if unaware of what I was doing, my hand drifted lower and brushed over my nipple. The stranger's eyes darted around the bus, looking to see if anyone else was watching. I knew they weren't, the bus was almost empty and the people who were on it ignored everyone else. That was the way of it on a city bus.

His eyes swung back to me and stayed glued to my hand as I lazily teased my hard nipple. My blood heated at my own naughty behavior, and I opened my eyes to watch him watch me. He was so entranced with my actions that he didn't even notice me watching him. So I brought my hand up to brush the damp curls back from my temple again, and his eyes locked on to mine.

Letting my hand drop back into my lap, I waited to see what his reaction would be. He just shrugged and smiled sheepishly at me. And I couldn't help but flirt some more. Reveling in the delicious fire coursing through my veins, I discreetly tugged my skirt up a bit higher on my thighs.

He saw the movement, and his eyes twinkled and his smile grew. Making a production of folding his paper and placing it across his lap, he settled back deeper into his seat as if preparing to watch a show. The thrill of the tease raced through me, and I snuggled my butt deeper into the bench and prepared to give him one.

Letting my fingers run in light circles over my thighs, I spread my knees a bit farther apart and slipped my hands between my thighs. Rubbing them up and down dragged my skirt a bit higher every time my hands came up. His eyes remained glued to my fingers and I brought my skirt to the top of my thighs the next time, allowing him a brief glimpse of the dark curls there before pulling my skirt down again. His shocked eyes jumped to mine and I smiled devilishly at him.

"Yes, I'm a naughty girl. I have no panties on," I told him with my eyes. *"Would you like to see more?"*

"Please."

Placing my hands square on my thighs, I slowly walked my fingers upward. My skirt gathered in my fingers and rose higher on my thighs until I slid my butt forward a bit more on the seat so he could get a good look at my naked pussy.

Heart pounding in my chest, I continued to tease him, and myself. I slid one hand under the edge of my skirt and trailed my fingertips over my swollen lips. I watched the Adams apple bob in his throat as he watched me play. Stiffening one finger I slipped it easily between my lips and into my wet hole.

A sigh escaped my parted lips and I let my head fall back against the window and my eyes drift shut again. I didn't have to see him watching me to know he was. The weight of his gaze was more tantalizing than a touch could ever be.

Once my eyes slid shut, I began to relax and get into it. I slid my stiffened finger in and out of myself slowly. The palm of my hand pressed rhythmically against my clit, bringing me to the edge fast. The slight sound of rustling paper drew my attention, and I peeked to see what he was doing. My audience had shifted his position and now had one hand under the newspaper covering his lap. Opening my eyes fully, I smiled encouragingly at him. The noise of the rustling paper wasn't enough to draw attention, and I imagined him rubbing himself through his pants trying to keep his movements to a minimum.

The thought of him stroking himself surreptitiously made the inner walls of my cunt clench and a small surprise orgasm swept through me. I widened my thighs more, lifted my hips off the bench, and pressed down on my clit with my palm, stretching the orgasm out as long as I could.

When I looked over at my audience again, he was sitting statue still, just staring, not between my thighs, but at my face. I blushed a bit, shocked at my own behavior.

What the hell was I thinking? I wasn't thinking—that was the whole point. I'd never even masturbated in front of Grant before and here I'd just done it for a stranger!

No. I did it for myself. I pulled my skirt down before I noticed that we weren't on the freeway anymore. Shit! I'd missed my stop.

I reached up and pulled the cord to alert the driver that I wanted off the bus and with three steps I was at the door. Surprisingly, the businessman fished in his pocket and then held out a business card.

The bus rolled to a stop and the back doors swung open.

"Sweet dreams," I whispered before stepping off the bus.

I'd left him there with the business card still in his hand, and a stiff cock in his lap. I didn't care about him. I cared about the way I felt, and the fact that for the second time, a stranger had made me feel more sexy and exciting than my husband.

ChapterSix

Grant came out of the house, carrying two beers, just as I hit our driveway. When he saw me with my heels in hand, walking barefoot, he shook his head. "You should've called when you were done work. I would've come to pick you up."

"It's all right, the bus ride wasn't that bad. I just missed my stop." I tried not to blush as I said this.

He came over and kissed me hello. I reached for one of the cold beers in his hand and had just taken a long pull from the bottle, when a second man stepped out of the house, wiping his hands on a rag.

Grant put an arm around my shoulders and handed the stranger the other beer. "This is my wife, Bethany, Jason. Bethany, this is Jason Lloyd, the new transfer from back East. When he heard me talking to you about the car troubles, he offered to help me give it a little tune-up for you."

"Nice to meet you, Jason."

"Pleasure's mine, ma'am." His voice was deep and husky, with a slight accent that made my insides quiver in acknowledgment. We shook hands and I tried not to be too obvious in my once-over.

He wasn't especially handsome or good-looking, but his body was fantastic. Both men were shirtless in the heat, and while Grant has a good body, muscular and strong, this guy had a trim, lean look. There was just a hint of muscles that rippled beneath the surface with his every move. Maybe it was the pierced nipples that got me going. Or the fact that I couldn't help but remember my second boyfriend, who had a similar build, and a super-long cock.

Heat flooded my insides and I took another long pull on the beer. I was turning into a real pervert.

"Does this mean you're cooking tonight?" I looked up at Grant, ignoring the low throb that had started in my groin.

"The car is fixed and we were just going to put the tools away before taking steaks out back to the grill." He nuzzled my neck for a second then whispered in my ear. "You look like you could use a shower, and maybe some help in that shower?"

Over Grant's shoulder I saw Jason watching us. He didn't bother hiding that he was watching, and even though I doubted he could hear what Grant had said, it was obvious he knew it was something sexual because his lips tilted at one corner and his chocolate eyes traveled lazily over my figure.

I reached down and palmed my husband's firm ass. Lord, it felt so good to have him teasing me and being playful again. With a long squeeze, I gave him a slow erotic kiss, teasing him with my lips and tongue. His dick started to harden against my hip and I pulled away reluctantly.

"You and your friend clean this up and start the grill. I'll clean myself up and make a salad." I walked backward for a few steps, then winked at him before turning and heading into the house.

"Very nice." I heard Jason say to Grant, and a surge of pride whipped through me.

I dashed up the stairs two at a time. It was so wonderful to see Grant being more like himself again. My dismal thoughts of being in a rut were obviously an overreaction. He'd been working way too hard lately, but he was still the same man I'd married.

Jason seemed pretty easygoing. Since Grant wasn't hanging out much with his old friends—I don't think he'd even been to one of their weekly Sunday basketball games for over a month—it might be good for him to have a new guy friend. Someone who understood his new job and could talk about it with him, but someone who also knew how to relax.

I stripped off my sundress and stepped under the shower spray. As I lathered up and started to rinse the sticky sweat from the hot day off, I remembered the way Jason had watched us kiss. The interest in his gaze was real, and it had fired up my imagination.

Through the kitchen window I could see the two men beside the built-in brick barbecue at the edge of the deck, drinking beer and chatting away. What a shame that both of them had donned shirts. The sun was going down and they'd lit citronella candles to keep the mosquitoes away, and classic rock blared from the portable stereo on the deck.

I stuck my head out the patio door and called to Grant, "Put these on the grill too."

He turned and caught the foil packages full of veggies and garlic butter I lobbed at him before ducking back into the kitchen. Once the salad was made, I grabbed three more beers from the fridge and went back outside in time to hear Jason mention he'd been in Vancouver for a month, and had yet to go anywhere but his hotel and the office.

"It's nice to know my husband isn't the only one working so hard." I handed them each a cold bottle. "Are you two on the same project?"

"Yeah. I head up the digital art facet of it, so Grant's sort of my boss on this one. Has he told you about it?" Jason's blue eyes lit up and he started rambling on about pixels and a bunch of other stuff that flew right over my head.

Grant stood behind him at the grill, grinning. He knew I was lost when it came to all that computer stuff, and he obviously thought it was funny that my politeness had gotten me into a conversational minefield I couldn't find my way out of.

Sometimes politeness wasn't the right tack.

"Interesting," I interrupted when he paused for a breath. "But I haven't a clue what you just told me."

He chuckled and gave me a sly wink. "Most people don't, but it usually impresses the girls."

My pulse jumped at his wink. "I'm duly impressed," I said with a smile.

"Hey! Stop flirting with my wife or you won't get any dinner."

Shit, if he thought that was flirting I wonder what he'd think of my show on the bus. Unease tightened my chest for just a moment, before I shook it off. I hadn't done anything wrong. Wrong would've been if I'd taken the stranger's business card after the show.

When we'd bought the house, there was already an old wooden picnic table in the backyard, so we hadn't bothered to pick out any patio furniture besides the two loungers we used to soak up the sun occasionally. Once we were seated around the picnic table, Grant placed a plate in front of each of us. Mine held a decent-size piece of steak, but the men's were ridiculous.

My eyebrows raised and I spoke without thinking. "Do you think it's big enough, Grant?"

With an exaggerated leer, Grant replied in a mock stage whisper, "You've never complained about the size of my meat before, darlin'."

"I'm not complaining, *darlin'*. But how big it is doesn't matter if you don't do anything with it."

The words hung in the silence for a split second before Grant grabbed me by the back of my neck and pulled me backward into a dip, my butt still on the seat, my back hovering above the grass as he planted his lips on mine and kissed me until I wrapped my arms around his neck and moaned hungrily.

Then he set me back in my seated position, and accepted the high-five from a laughing Jason while I fanned myself dramatically. "Suddenly, I'm more hungry than I thought possible."

That set the tone for a dinner full of laughter and ribald jokes. The men were clearly bonding, and I was loving the fact that it felt like my husband was back. When the food was gone, we carried our plates into the kitchen and cleanup was simple and easy.

The last of the dishes were soaking in the sink while I sat on the sofa and Grant stood at the front door saying good-night to Jason.

Husky male chuckles echoed through the house, and my insides quivered.

From a distance, the two men looked like complete opposites. Grant with his midnight hair and muscular body and Jason with his dirty-blond waves and slim physique. But while we were eating, I'd noted the similarities. Both men had easy smiles and way too much charm.

Jason had an almost wholesome look to him. If it hadn't been for the tribal tattoo I'd spotted on his back before he'd donned his shirt again, I'd almost be convinced he was a good boy. Okay, the nipple piercings were another hint. And the gleam in his eye whenever he saw Grant kiss or touch me.

Jason was obviously a good guy, with something of a bad boy inside him. And I bet that, like Grant, when he fell in love he'd be extremely loyal.

And that gave me an idea.

ChapterSeven

You wanna do what?"

The expression on Ginger's pretty face was priceless. Eyes wide and jaw dropped, she stared at me like I'd just announced I was giving birth to puppies.

"I want to set you up on a date with one of Grant's coworkers."

"No way." Her earrings flew as she shook her head.

"Why not?"

She sneered at me. "He's working at that marketing firm now, right? In an office, in a suit, behind a desk. You know those types aren't for me."

"Grant isn't that 'type' and he works in the same office." I gathered up the invoices from the new inventory and filed them away. "You might be surprised."

"I got the feeling from you the other day that Grant was changing?" She eyed me from her position leaning against the office doorframe. "That he was getting uptight and boring."

"He's just been working really hard since he changed jobs. But things are looking up again. He brought Jason over to help him fix my car last night, and he was like his old self—playful, flirty, relaxed. Jason stayed for dinner with us, and I really think you'll like him, Ginger. Plus, what have you got to lose? He's single, sexy, and new in town."

"I don't know about this."

"Trust me. You'll like him."

W hat?" Grant glared at me from his spot on the sofa. He was already settled there when I got home from work that night, papers spread out across the coffee table, a football game on TV. He'd just grunted when I'd said hi, but my question had gotten his full attention.

I kicked off my sandals and dropped onto the cushions next to him. "Jason's single, right?" I had to be sure.

"What's it to you?" His eyes darkened. "I saw you flirting with him the other night, Beth, and that's fine. You've always been a flirt. But don't think for even a minute that I'd let you get away with anything more than that."

"I wasn't flirting with him, Grant, I was flirting with *you*. And, I have to admit, I was pleasantly surprised when you finally noticed!"

He tossed the sheaf of papers he'd been reading on the table. "What's that supposed to mean?"

I could see he was gearing up for a fight, and I really didn't want one. I leaned closer and cupped his cheek, rubbing my thumb over his tight lips. "It just means you've been so damn busy at work, and so tired when you get home, that I was starting to wonder if you even knew I was here half the time."

"That's just silly, of course I know you're here. Securing a strong future for us is the reason I took this new job."

I sighed. Did I really want to talk about this? Grant was a true man. He just didn't get things sometimes.

"My head knows that's why you took it, but sometimes I wonder if it's worth it. If by the time you're settled into the new job the magic between us will be completely gone."

"You think the magic between us is gone?" Shutters dropped in his eyes and his voice evened out. Grant was the master of shutting people out when he wanted to.

I hated it when he hid from me, and I wasn't about to let him get away with it. This was too important. I planted my hands on his shoulders and pushed him back against the sofa. Once I'd straddled his lap, I kissed him softly and steadily until his hands gripped my waist and his breathing was ragged. "Not gone forever, just taking a little vacation."

He bit his lip for a moment, his gaze roaming my features, reading my sincerity. "And you think flirting with my coworker is going to bring it back?"

Uh-oh.

"No. I told you. It wasn't him that had me all flustered and hot last night. It was you. You were so macho and relaxed, almost like yourself again."

"Then why do you want to know if he's single?"

"I want to set him up with Ginger."

Grant threw back his head and laughed.

When he was done laughing, I smiled at him, my fingers playing with the little hairs curling around his nipples. Did he suspect I'd become a bit of an exhibitionist?

"What did you think I was going to do?" I asked cautiously.

"Never mind." He shook his head. "My imagination was just running away with me. Ginger, huh?"

"Yeah."

"Don't you think she'd be a bit much for a suit like him?"

"Grant, he's pierced and tattooed. He may wear a suit at the office, like *you do* I might add, but he's definitely got something wild going on in him too. I think he'd be perfect for her."

"I don't know, babe. I don't think I know him well enough to set him up on a date."

"Please?" I wiggled my butt in his lap, feeling heat spread through me as his erection grew under me. "I'd owe you."

"Yeah? Just what would you owe me?"

"Whatever you want." I breathed the last word out softly as my lips slanted across his once again.

His hands slid up my thighs under my dress, his tongue dancing with mine as I rubbed against him.

He hummed his pleasure when he found I had no panties on under my dress, his hands cupping my butt cheeks and squeezing.

"You naughty thing. You're naked under here."

"It's too hot out for clingy underwear." I nuzzled against his neck and nipped at his ear, my hands traveling over his bare chest to his lap.

"You mean *you're* too hot." He lifted his hips and I tugged at his gym shorts until his naked cock was in my hand.

Our heavy breathing echoed in the living room as I sat back on his knees. He tugged the neckline of my sundress down until my breasts popped free and he cupped them, holding each one up as his tongue ran over the rigid tips, his teeth grazing my nipples, first one then the other, driving me just a little bit crazy.

I shifted again until the head of his cock was poised at my entrance. "We're hot," I said, and impaled myself on him.

Passionate groans and sighs filled the room as Grant abandoned my breasts and gripped my pumping hips. Normally in this position, I liked to take it slow, to feel every inch of him as he slid in and out of my body. To tease us both with just how erotic and sensual we could be.

But this time, I didn't want that. This time I ground down and felt him go deep. My clit brushed against his pubic bone, and darts of pleasure shot through my body. I put my hands on the wall behind him and leaned forward, my forehead against his as I rotated my hips, grinding down on him as my insides pulsed and clutched at his cock.

Grant grunted, pushing up into me, and his hands reached between my legs from behind. I felt his fingers stroking the stretched skin where we were connected, then a digit pushing at the puckered hole of my anus. I ground down one last time, as his finger breached my ass and pleasure exploded within me. My pussy spasmed, squeezing his cock as he came, throbbing and twitching inside me.

My bones liquefied by my orgasm, I collapsed on top of Grant. "That was nice."

"Nice?" Grant chuckled and ran a hand over my back.

"Yeah. It's only better than nice when you do all the work."

While Grant might've missed a lot of hints lately, he didn't miss that one. With a laughing groan, he struggled to his feet, holding me in his arms, and carried me upstairs.

ChapterEight

A week went by, and the temperatures evened out so that the days were still hot, but the cool evenings told of the approaching fall. Yet, I still found myself favoring light sundresses and flirty skirts with no panties.

Grant was still a workaholic, although he was trying to be more attentive. Whenever I initiated sexual contact, he was up for it, even if it made him late for work. While I think my comment about the magic being on vacation might've prompted him to be more alert to my overtures, he still wasn't making any of his own. And that hurt.

"It's not like I want him to bring flowers home from work every night or anything," I said to Ginger as I leaned on the cash counter of the boutique.

"Then what do you want? I mean, from what you've said he's trying to make things right. He even agreed to setting me up with Jason to please you."

"I'd like him to make an effort. It's not just the sex, it's everything. He comes home from work and sits at the kitchen table working. Or else he's already asleep on the sofa. His body is around more, but his mind still isn't. How'd last night go anyway?"

It had been a busy day in the shop, and I hadn't had time to question her about her coffee date with Jason yet. Ginger needed to leave soon and I had to do more work, but for the moment, we were enjoying the lull.

Ginger pulled her backpack on and stared at me thoughtfully. "Have you tried talking to him about it again?"

"What do I say? *Honey, I need you to pay attention to me. Flirt with me, make me feel pretty and loved.*" I tried to laugh and it came out as a snort of derision. "Yeah, that'll go over real well."

"If it's how you feel, you should tell him."

"I'll think about it. His big pitch meeting is in three days so I'll wait and see what happens, maybe things will get better after that."

A couple of seconds passed while I watched Ginger examine the jewelry display next to the cash register. "So? Are you going to tell me about last night with Jason or do I have to call him?"

Just then the bell tinkled, announcing a new customer. "Hi there," I greeted the man who had entered the shop.

He smiled in return and started to browse the stands nearest the door. Probably gift shopping for his wife.

"You were right." She shrugged. "He was nice. Cute too."

I watched her get her stuff ready to leave. Her cheeks were coloring just a bit, and she wouldn't look at me. "What? That's it? You're not going to give me details?"

She finally looked at me. "I've got to run now. I'll talk to you more tomorrow." With a small wave and a teasing smile, Ginger turned and walked away.

"I'm going to phone him and ask for details!" I called out at her back.

She turned and sent me a wink, but kept on moving.

Would it be too pushy to call Jason up and see how things went? I wondered as I watched the lone male customer go from rack to rack. I really should help him. He was looking a little lost.

"Can I help you find anything?"

He looked up with such a grateful expression that I fairly skipped across the floor to assist him.

Chapter Nine

You mean to tell me he asked you out again and you said no?" My fingers tightened around the phone. "Ginger! You said you wanted a man who wanted more than to just get laid, and I hand you one and you turn him down!"

The early afternoon sun beat down on my topless form, lulling me enough so that instead of throwing the phone across the yard at the high privacy fence in reaction to my friend's stubbornness, I just leaned back in the lounger and reached for my drink. The glass of ice water was slick with condensation, and it felt amazingly great when I rested it on my bare belly after taking a drink.

It was Friday afternoon and my day off from the boutique. Normally, I worked Fridays and had weekends off, but there was a fashion show Samair wanted to attend Saturday so I'd agreed to give her the day off, as long as she helped Ginger out at the store on Friday instead.

Grant was at work, and I was lying topless on a lounger in the backyard soaking up the summer sun. And listening to Ginger whine about wanting a real man, a sexy one.

"You didn't find Jason sexy?" I heard a curse echo across the yard and opened my eyes to see a man hanging on the telephone pole across the street. Looking directly at me.

Instinctively, I jerked upright, and my drink splashed on my belly. I quickly put the drink on the small table next to me and turned my back on the watcher. Then, despite the heat, a shiver danced down my spine and my soft puffy nipples beaded to sensitive pebbles.

"Beth?"

"Oh, sorry, Ginger." I lay back on the lounger, peeking up at the phone repair guy. "A bee buzzed by and startled me. What did you say?"

"I said he was a nice guy, but no, I didn't find him particularly sexy."

"Would you find him sexy if I told you he has a hot tattoo and his nipples are pierced?"

Speaking of nipples. I laid a hand on my belly and slowly moved it up, dragging my fingernails across the rigid peak of one breast. When the phone repairman looked over again, I was rolling my nipple between my finger and thumb. His hands stilled, his entire body frozen in place.

"He has pierced nipples?" The surprise in Ginger's voice was clear.

"Uh hmmm." Pleasure was heating me from the inside out now, making it hard to concentrate on the conversation. "Ginger? I have to go for now, but think about Jason. There's more to him than meets the eye, I promise you that."

"How do you know that, though?"

"I just do. I recognized the same thing in Grant. Call it instinct, radar or whatever, but that guy will surprise you. I just know it."

Ginger's derisive snort was loud and clear over the phone. "I doubt it, not many men surprise me. Not in a good way anyway."

"We're going to change that, okay? Call me when you get home from work."

I turned off the phone and set it down deliberately. With both hands empty, I was free to take my peep show a step further. I'd been daydreaming about masturbating for a stranger, I mean *really* masturbating, ever since the little show on the bus. Finding a way to do it had been impossible, especially since when I thought about going out to deliberately find a place or a stranger for the purpose of it, guilt would tickle the back of my mind.

However, the opportunity to really let go had just fallen into place. Grant was at work, our backyard was fenced so no neighbors would see me, and the stranger was across the street and up a telephone pole, watching. How much better could it get?

He was far enough away that I felt completely safe, yet close enough that I could see that he had gloves on his hands and a grin on his face. Which meant he'd be able to see what I was going to do perfectly.

I closed my eyes and started to run both my hands over my torso. Fingertips circled my belly button, tickled my ribs, skimmed across the underside of my breasts. I squeezed my inner muscles and a small spasm of pleasure rippled throughout my body.

In my mind's eye, I imagined the telephone repairman was closer.

Standing at the foot of the lounger. That his heavy breathing would be loud in my ears as I cupped my breasts and tweaked my nipples. That when I slid one hand down over my soft belly and slipped it beneath my bikini bottoms, I could hear the rustle of his jeans being unzipped.

My finger slipped between slick pussy lips and found my swollen clit. I flicked my fingertip back and forth over the button, pinched a hard nipple with the other hand, and my back arched in pleasure. I peeked out from under my lashes and saw that the repairman had relaxed back in his harness and was watching the show.

The naughty devil inside made me open my eyes and flash him a wicked grin as I spread my thighs and slid a hand lower. A stiff finger entered my sex, and the palm of my hand centered over my clit. Bracing my feet on the lounger, I pressed my hips up, rotating them against my hand, filling myself and putting the pressure right where I needed it.

A moan of pleasure slipped from my lips, and I let my head fall back, eyes closed, and my hips picked up speed. My heart raced, and my pulse pounded heavily in my ears as my insides tightened. Ripples of pleasure expanded and every muscle in my body tensed in anticipation. The whisper of a moan that wasn't my own echoed through the yard and my insides clenched.

"You are so hot."

A scream leapt from my throat and I jerked upright, smacking into a hard male chest. Hands gripped my arms and pushed me back onto the lounger and firm lips covered mine.

Grant's familiar flavor had me groaning and pushing against him as he settled his hips against mine. His hard cock was already out of his pants and was sandwiched against my belly as we frantically rubbed against each other. I ripped my mouth away from his and tilted my head back. His mouth zeroed in on the sensitive spot between my neck and my collarbone, and more pleasure sounds leapt from my lips.

When I looked over his shoulder, I could see that the repairman was enjoying this new development almost as much as I was.

Grant's hand snuck between us, and he shoved the crotch of my bottoms to the side and dipped a finger inside.

"You are so hot. I can't stop myself." His words had barely left his mouth when his cock found my entrance and he thrust home. I wrapped my legs around his hips, my arms around his shoulders, and held on as he pumped fast and furious, deep and true.

Pressing my cheek against his, I urged him on with raunchy words. "Yes, fuck me, Grant. Faster, harder. More, I want more cock."

I sounded like a bad porn movie and I didn't care. My eyes were glued to the stranger watching us and I knew he could hear me. And that pushed me over the edge.

My cunt clenched around Grant's cock and I screamed as waves of pleasure spread outward from our connection, touching every nerve ending in my body. Grant's hoarse shout of relief blended with the echoes of my cry and warmth blanketed my mind.

I'm not sure how long it was before Grant's weight shifted and I opened my eyes, but when we moved again, my body was almost boneless in its satisfaction.

"That was intense," Grant whispered and placed a soft kiss on the tip of my nose.

I placed a hand against his clean-shaven cheek and ran my thumb over his bottom lip. "I thought you were at work?"

"I forgot some papers at home and had to come back to get them." He grinned. "And I am so glad I did."

Before I could stop myself, my eyes drifted over his shoulder to see if our audience was still there. He was. And my gaze must've lingered for a moment too long because Grant was already tensing when I returned my gaze to him.

Without a word, he shifted his weight and looked over his shoulder. He saw the repairman shimmying down the telephone pole and swung his puzzled gaze back to me.

Realization dawned and he slowly climbed off me.

"Grant . . ." I started to speak, but I didn't know what to say.

"You knew he was there," he spoke as he tucked his dress shirt back in and zipped his trousers. "You knew that guy was there the whole time, even before I got here. Didn't you?"

"I . . ." My heart jumped into my throat and my mind went blank. What could I say?

Grant stared at me, his beautiful eyes full of confusion, hurt, and something I couldn't quite define. He swiped a rough hand through his hair and shook his head at me. "Damn it, Bethany!"

I swung my legs over the edge of the lounger, but Grant had stormed off before my feet touched the grass. I stood and started to go after him, but stopped at the patio doors when I heard his car start with a roar of the engine.

He was gone.

Chapter Ten

I didn't know what to do. Get dressed and follow him back to his office? Call him?

But what would I say? What could I say?

I'd known the repairman was there before I even began to play with myself.

Do I tell him about the bus incident? How much should I tell him?

Shit! I didn't even know how it all started.

I knew why though.

Utter emotional exhaustion had me asleep on the sofa by eight o'clock that night. I'd decided to give us both some time to think before seeing each other again so I hadn't called him, or tried to visit him. Part of me knew it was cowardly, but I couldn't help it.

I also couldn't help but hope that he would blow off work and come home and talk to me. I didn't want to have to ask him to do it; I just wanted him to take the initiative himself.

Ginger called a little after six. She'd just gotten home from work and was eager to find out more about Jason, but instead of talking about him, I burst into tears and told her everything.

"Bethany," she scolded. "You cannot take all the blame for this situation. You flashed a guy on the bus and put a bit of a tease show on for some anonymous repairman. You didn't fuck anyone. You didn't cheat. You just wanted a bit of attention. Your dumbass husband wasn't giving you any, so you found it elsewhere."

I sniffed. "He's not a dumbass."

"Well, other than that, am I wrong?"

She wasn't. But when I hung up with her, I admitted to myself that it didn't matter if she was right or wrong. What mattered was the expression on Grant's face when he'd put two and two together.

More tears soaked the pillow I clutched as I cried myself to sleep.

A change in the atmosphere around me brought me awake slowly. I lay frozen on the sofa as I listened for some telltale sound. When I heard nothing, I opened my eyes and saw Grant in the club chair across from me. He rested an open bottle of beer on his thigh and stared at me. Silent and unreadable.

The room was dark, lit only by the flickering screen of the muted television as we stared at each other for a long moment. My heart pounded, setting the butterflies in my stomach fluttering madly as I waited for what would happen next. Before I could lose my nerve, I sat up and ran my fingers through my hair. "Grant, I never—"

"I don't want to hear about what you never did. I want to hear about what you *did* do." His voice was quiet.

Firm, though.

It was a tone of voice he used with others, but never with me. The way he spoke to one of his subordinates at work when he expected immediate results.

It was a voice not to be argued with, and it lit an unexpected spark of lust in my belly. "I, umm . . . was tanning in the backyard, you know I always tan topless when I can, and the heat made me feel pretty hot, and my thoughts were getting sexy and I started to play with myself. When I saw the repairman watching, I didn't stop."

I tucked my fingers under my legs to keep from fidgeting under his steady stare.

"So you were already masturbating when you saw him?"

"No," I whispered. I couldn't lie to him. "I saw him watching me first, and it made me feel sexy and attractive, so I did it to tease him."

From under my lashes I monitored Grant's reaction. All he did was nod, and take a drink of his beer. "Was it the first time you've done something like that?"

I shook my head.

"Look at me, Bethany."

I raised my head and met his fiery gaze. He was aroused!

My heart jumped and relief mixed with the tendrils of lust curling around my insides.

"Tell me about the other times," he commanded.

Sitting up a little straighter, I told him about the roofer.

"When was that?"

"Two weeks ago."

"You didn't masturbate for him?"

I shook my head, trying to ignore the way my pussy had grown slick with just the retelling of my exploits. "It was more for me than for him. Just knowing that he was watching me, that he thought I was attractive and sexy was enough. It made me *feel* sexy and attractive."

Grant's lips thinned at that. "I'm sorry."

What? "You're sorry? What for?"

"For not paying enough attention to you. For not letting you know every day that I think you're the most beautiful woman alive." He took another drink of beer and gave me a hard look. "But that doesn't excuse what you've done."

"I know, and I'm sorry too. I really am." The familiar taste of tears filled my throat and I swallowed, trying to maintain control of my emotions.

His eyes softened, the fiery green turning to the soft lush color of freshly cut grass as he nodded his acceptance of my apology. And that little bit of softness showed me I hadn't screwed things up too badly.

When he spoke again, his voice was firm. "Is that it? Just those two times?"

I hesitated.

"Bethany. Tell me everything."

It was weird. Grant wasn't scolding me. I don't even think he was mad. Yet, something had certainly changed. "What's going on, Grant?"

"This isn't the time for questions, Bethany. This is the time for answers. I need honest answers from you." His lips tilted into a small smile.

I nodded slowly. "Okay, there was one other time. The day I took the bus home from work I teased the guy sitting across from me by lifting my skirt and flashing him." Heat flushed my cheeks. I wasn't sure why I was embarrassed now, but I was.

"Is that why you've taken to not wearing panties?"

"No. I stopped wearing them when I realized how sexy it made me feel to go without. Being able to flash him was just a . . . bonus, I guess."

"You mean naughty, don't you?"

"Excuse me?"

"You said it made you feel sexy to go without underwear, but you meant naughty didn't you? It made you feel like a bad girl?" A midnight eyebrow quirked.

A quiver rippled over my muscles. Without thinking anymore, my head bobbed slowly up and down on my neck. Naughty. Yes, that was it.

"And you know what happens when naughty girls get caught misbehaving, right?"

The stern note grew stronger in Grant's voice, and a tinge of huskiness was added. Our gazes locked and my brain kicked into gear.

My playful husband was gone, and in his place was a dominant master. A man that wanted to make me pay for my licentious behavior in the most wicked ways.

Chapter Eleven

A shiver danced down my spine at the look in his eyes. Grant had never hidden the fact that he'd been a real bad boy before he met me. He'd never told me the specific details of his "adventures" as he called them . . . but just looking at him now told me they were more than I'd ever imagined.

"Bethany?"

I gave my head a shake to get rid of the pounding in my ears. "What?"

"Do you know what happens to naughty girls that misbehave?"

Uh-oh.

"They get punished?"

"Oh, yes they do. And you were very naughty, weren't you?"

I wiggled in my seat, unsure of how to handle the rapid response my body was having to his words. The very *positive* rapid response. "Umm, yes?"

He set his beer bottle on the end table next to him and gestured me to him. "Come over here and accept your punishment like a good girl."

I stood on wobbly legs and took a step toward him.

"No."

I froze, looking at him in surprise. "On your knees," he said softly.

His command was all the more devastating in its softness. He knew I would obey even before I did.

After lowering myself to the ground, I shuffled over to him on my knees. When I stopped, I wanted to place my hands on his legs and feel the ripple of his muscles beneath them. But I didn't. Instinctively I knew to wait for his next order.

"Take off your dress and lay yourself across my lap."

With one move, I was naked. Grant shifted forward in the chair a bit, and I stretched over his knees, belly down. His hard-on pressed tellingly against my left side, but he made no move to undo his trousers. His hand ran lightly over my bare backside, and a shudder ripped through me.

"Oh, you really do need more attention, don't you?" He crooned as he rubbed my cheeks a bit harder. When his hand suddenly dipped between my thighs and a finger slipped into my wetness, he chuckled, talking so softly, as if to himself. "Oh yeah, this is going to work out just fine. I can't believe I never guessed."

I put my hands on the floor and levered my weight in an attempt to get up. "Guessed what?"

A heavy hand pinned me across his knees. "Don't speak without permission, Bethany."

With that, his hand landed sharply on my ass.

I tensed, expecting pain. But none came.

Then another smack, and another. Each one just a little sharper, a little harder than the last.

The urge to push against him, to fight him and stand up, was nothing but a quick flash. I deserved this. I deserved to be punished for what I'd done, for not telling Grant what I'd been doing. For not *making* him pay more attention to me.

I deserved the attention he was giving me now.

My bum was hot and the heat was spreading fast. I squeezed my thighs together, and my nipples brushed against the fabric of his pants as I shifted on his knees.

"Stop squirming," Grant said as he delivered three slaps in quick succession.

A soft moan slipped from my lips as I felt my insides clench. My surroundings were fading fast, dissolved by the pleasure coursing through my veins.

I squeezed my thighs together again and pressed my hips against Grant's knees. If I could only rub my sex against him a little, I'd come.

"I said stop squirming." Three more slaps, faster and harder than the others, landed on my cheeks.

Grant did not let up. He kept spanking me, strong and steady, while my breathing became harsh, and my fingers dug into the carpet to keep me from reaching back and covering myself. His hand landed on one cheek then the other, sometimes straight on, sometimes angled upward from lower behind, to target the tender curve where butt met thigh.

My ass was on fire, and the flames were licking at my clit and my nipples and everything in between. Grant knew me and my body well enough that he recognized the signs of an approaching orgasm.

"You. Do. Not. Get. To. Come."

Each word was punctuated with a slap and by the end, tears were streaming from my eyes and I was humping at Grant's leg. I was so close, so close to feeling that fire explode and engulf me in a blanket of hot ecstasy. My fingers disentangled from the carpet and reached mindlessly toward my sex.

"No." Grant pushed my arms away.

Large hands cupped my shoulders and lifted me up and away from him. Then I was straddling his knees, my tender ass cheeks throbbing, while my frantic hands reached for his belt as passionate whimpers escaped from my lips.

Large hands clamped down on mine and stilled my movements. When I looked up into Grant's blazing green eyes, I was ready to beg. But before the words could be pushed past my lips, he spoke. "From now on you will not show any man any part of your naked body without my permission. Is that understood?"

I nodded quickly.

"I asked you, is that understood, Bethany?"

"Yes," I whispered.

His hands tightened around mine. "Yes, what?"

"Yes . . . sir?"

"That's my girl." The soft kiss he pressed to my lips was a precious reward.

Then he spoke again. "And you will not masturbate unless I say you can. Is that understood?"

"Yes, sir."

"You are mine to touch, to tease, to play with, and to use whenever I want. Is that understood?"

"Yes, sir." The words rolled naturally from my tongue. My tears had stopped and my heart was pounding. Our gazes were locked and I finally felt like I'd found my place in the world. The place where *we* as a couple fit perfectly.

"Now, you took your punishment pretty good for the first time. So you deserve a reward." He stood up and stepped away from the chair. When he was in the middle of the room he lowered me until my feet touched the floor. "Now, get on your knees and undo my pants."

Chapter Twelve

I skimmed my hands over his thighs on my way to his waist. His erection had made a nice tent in his trousers and my hands itched to cup him. I made quick work of his belt and zipper, then gripped the waistband of his boxers and pants, and pulled them both down together. He stepped out of the materials and stood with feet slightly apart.

Skimming my hands over his muscular legs, I gripped his firm butt and pulled him forward. I opened my mouth, eager to taste him only to have him pull away. "Turn around and get on all fours, baby."

Oh, yes! My pussy spasmed in anticipation and I swung around. My hands were planted shoulder-width apart with my knees spread. I looked over my shoulder to see Grant throw his shirt on the chair before he placed a broad hand between my shoulder blades and pushed slowly and firmly down. "Forehead on the floor, baby. I'm going to show you what I like."

I didn't know I could get so excited again so fast. Earlier I'd been almost mindless with my lust for him, but the lust had calmed when he'd held my hands and spoken to me. Now it was rushing back full force.

With my forehead against the carpet, I used my elbows to keep my balance as he ran his hands down my back, over my hip to where he patted my still tender cheeks. He kicked my knees farther apart and pushed against the small of my back. "Arch your back. I want to see everything from here."

Like a bitch in heat, I did as he asked. A thrill ran through me when a low groan of appreciation echoed through the room.

"This is the position I want you to assume when I ask you to present to me. I want you to present your pussy and your ass to me so that I can punish you, or pleasure you." Fingers tangled gently in my hair and lifted my head up until our eyes met. "Do you understand?"

"Yes, sir." God! I couldn't think. I didn't want to think. Sensations swarmed every nerve ending in my body and had shut my brain down. It all felt so good. To just sink into the mindless pleasure that this man could give to me.

"You look so hot, such a pretty pink pussy just waiting to be filled." He ran a finger over my slit, and a tremor went through me.

"And I'm the only one who will *ever* do that." He got down on his knees behind me and aimed his cock at my entrance. "You're mine."

With one fast, hard thrust he filled me up and I squealed. His fingers dug into my hips, and his belly slapped at my sensitive butt as he pumped fast and furious.

"You are mine. My lover. My wife," he chanted as he fucked me so hard and deep that I thought we'd never be separate again.

I braced myself, digging my hands into the carpet, pushing back against him. I loved every second of the fervent mating.

"Yes," I sobbed at the almost unbearable pleasure of his possession. That's what it was. He wasn't making love to me, he wasn't even fucking me. He was claiming me, possessing me in a way that I hadn't even known I needed. "Yours. I'm yours. Always."

The last word trailed off into an ecstatic cry of gratification as the fiery ball of lust inside me finally burst, and my entire body shook with pleasure. When my tremors slowed, Grant slammed into me one last time and held me tight. His cock swelled and throbbed, emptying into me while his own guttural cry filled the room.

Weak from satisfaction, I fell forward and stretched out on the carpet. Grant followed me down, covering my body with his. I could feel his heartbeat against my back as his chin rested on my shoulder, and his breath brushed my cheek.

Grant was still my husband, my lover, and my best friend. I'd never felt closer to him than I did in that moment.

Chapter Thirteen

Well, you look like the cat that got the cream," Ginger said smirking at me when I strolled into work the next morning. "Or should I say the pussy that gave up the cream?"

"Ginger!" I tried not to laugh. Really I did, but a chuckle still escaped. I was in such a good mood I was floating inches above the floor, and Ginger obviously noticed.

I dropped my purse off in the office and floated back to the front of the store. I was a few minutes late, and the store was already open, but we had no customers so Ginger was leaning against the service counter, killing time.

"Tell me you didn't get fucked good and hard last night," she said, with a smirk. "Is that how Grant reacted to your little exhibitionist adventures? With an insatiable hard-on?"

I raised an eyebrow in her direction before I pulled the sales reports from the day before from the printer. "You're in a wonderful mood. What happened?"

"Nothing special." Pink tinged her cheekbones.

A bark of laughter jumped from my lips. "Give me a break, Ginger. You're acting like you got some last night too."

When she wouldn't meet my gaze, my chest tightened. She'd wanted to talk last night, and I'd been too wrapped up in my own problems to listen. I wasn't sure it was a good thing if she went out and just picked up some guy last night. Not with the way she'd been feeling lately. "Did you get laid last night, Ginger?"

"No!" She shook her head then shrugged. "But after I talked to you I went to the bookstore. To get a photography book, you know? And when I was there I saw this guy in the mystery section. He had a great ass, and from behind he looked pretty hot. I was feeling a little lonely so I went over there thinking I'd flirt a little and see what happened."

"And?"

"And it was Jason."

She dropped her head to the counter in an effort to hide her blush.

"Ah-ha, I told you he was hot! Did you talk to him?" I smacked her on the shoulder. "Don't hide from me!"

"I did." She straightened away from the counter. "I asked him to have a drink with me at Smiley's."

Smiley's was Ginger's favorite watering hole. Only two blocks from her house it was a neighborhood pub that had been around for too long, and showed it.

To be blunt, it was a dive.

"Did he pass the test?"

"Flying colors. Even Jimmy liked him."

Jimmy was the bartender at the pub. Ginger figured if she took a guy to Smiley's, and he lasted the night without getting into a fight or making any rude comments about the décor, he was okay.

"When are you seeing him again?"

Her brow puckered and she looked away. "I don't know. We didn't make any plans, but I'm expecting him to call and ask me out soon though."

The phone under the counter rang and our eyes met, startled. With a laugh she answered it and shook her head at me before moving to the computer to check something for the caller.

I wondered if Jason would call again. She'd turned him down once, and some guys didn't like head games. Grant certainly didn't. Although, I was learning rapidly that he did have a knack for sex games.

The day went by fast. Saturdays usually did. The clientele on Saturdays was different from every other day of the week, and we didn't always have good sales numbers, but there were always lots of lookers. Lisa, who worked Saturdays only, came in the early afternoon to help Ginger on the floor, and I retreated to the office to get the paperwork for the week in order.

When I first sat down, there was only a slight flash of tenderness, but the longer I sat the more aware I became of how sensitive my ass cheeks were. And the more I thought about Grant's reaction the night before.

He'd been so . . . masterful.

I'd been expecting anger, maybe even yelling. I certainly hadn't expected him to decide that I needed to be kept in line with discipline and rewards like a naughty little girl.

Attention was what I'd wanted, and it had been what I'd gotten. If that morning was any indication, I could count on it continuing too.

Normally on Saturday mornings, Grant slept in before spending the afternoon at the office. It was the one day of the week that I was up and out of bed before him, because on Sundays we both slept in. But that morning, when I'd started to climb out of bed, Grant had grabbed my arm and pulled me back down. He'd rolled over on top of me, spread my legs, and slid inside. At first it had hurt a bit, because I wasn't ready for him. After a couple of strokes, with his lips brushing against my ear as he reminded me that I was *his*, I was slick with desire and urging him on.

The pain-pleasure had been an erotic surprise. As had his complete dominance the night before. We'd never been a kinky couple, not beyond trying a few different positions and locations within the house. And maybe the car once in a while. But things changed. Just thinking about some of the things he'd said, and the way he'd handled me, had me shifting in my seat and rubbing my thighs together.

Chapter Fourteen

When I got home from work, Grant was in the spare bedroom, the one we'd converted to an office when he got his promotion. He was working. My heart sank, and I shuffled past the office doorway on my way to the stairs, calling hello as I passed.

My shower was long and hot. I stood under the sharp spray with my eyes closed and head back, not thinking about anything. My mind was deliberately blank. I didn't want to think that things could go back to the way they had been so quickly. After smoothing lotion on my skin, I put shorts and a stretchy undershirt on and went back downstairs to the kitchen.

The ping of the microwave signaled that my leftover spaghetti was warm, and I grabbed it and set it on the table. My butt had just hit the chair when I heard Grant call my name from the office.

"Bethany, I'd like to see you in here, please."

My nipples hardened at his tone of voice. It was that same tone he'd used the night before when he'd been giving me instructions. Heart racing, I forgot all about my pasta and headed down the short hallway to the room at the end.

"Are you hungry?" I hoped not, but maybe he heard me getting ready to eat and decided he wanted dinner too.

He glanced up and pushed his chair away from the desk. "Come closer," he said softly. When I stood in front of him, a small smile formed on his lips and he reached for my hand. "Kneel in front of me."

I swallowed a gasp and lowered myself to the carpet. I was close enough that my breasts brushed his kneecaps and my eyes slid closed while I tried to steady my breathing. I was incredibly aroused already, my pulse throbbing heavily between my thighs.

He cupped my chin and lifted my face until I met his gaze. His voice was soft when he spoke, yet firm enough to wipe away any doubts that he was in charge. "I know this is new to you, so tonight's lesson will be a gentle one. When you get home and I'm already here, you are never to walk past me without a proper greeting. Understood?"

"I did greet you. I said hello." I did my best not to sound defensive.

"Saying hello as you walk past is not a proper greeting. From now on, I want a kiss hello from you every night."

"But you were working. I didn't want to bother you." I always thought he *wanted* to be left alone while he worked.

A midnight eyebrow raised sharply. "Are you arguing with me?"

My pulse jumped. "No, sir."

There was a brief pause while we looked into each other's eyes before he nodded and continued. "Excellent. I'd like you to make me come now."

I blinked.

The command startled me. I don't know why, since I was on my knees in front of him, ready and eager to do anything. But it did.

Before he could change his mind, or I could think about it too much, I reached for the waistband of his shorts and started to pull them down. Grant helped me by lifting his hips off the chair, but that was it. He sat back and didn't offer any more instructions or encouragement.

A little unsure of myself for the first time in years, I leaned forward and closed my eyes. I breathed deep and inhaled the scent of him. Musky, primal . . . male.

It went straight to my head, overtaking all of my senses. My surroundings disappeared and my mind went blank. All that mattered was the feel of his hard thighs beneath my hands and the knowledge that he was mine.

I shuffled closer. Close enough to lean forward and nuzzle my face against his groin. His cock was hard. Not as hard as it could get, but he was ready for me to take him in my mouth. Instead, I licked at the seam where his thigh met his groin, letting my hair brush across his sensitive skin. I pushed his thighs farther apart and took a swipe at his balls with my tongue as I switched to his other leg.

I felt, more than heard, him gasp. He slid forward on the chair a bit, spreading his thighs even farther for me. But I wasn't done.

After licking and nibbling at his inner thigh, I nuzzled his balls gently with my nose. After a long, slow lick with the flat of my tongue, I sucked the sac gently into my mouth. This time I heard

Sasha White

Grant's groan clearly. I circled the base of his cock with one hand and started stroking him while I rolled his balls lovingly around my mouth.

After a couple of seconds, Grant's fingers tangled in my hair, and he pulled me away and redirected my effort to his cock. "Stop teasing. I want you to make me come. Now."

In the past, when I performed oral sex on Grant, he always let me set the pace. His finger would play in my hair or tickle my ear, but not this time. This time his grip on my hair was solid, and he took complete charge.

With firm hands he cupped my head and pressed his cock against my lips until I opened my mouth. Slowly, he pushed me down, not stopping until my nose was buried in the tight curls at the base of his shaft and I was fighting my gag reflex. When his grip let up slightly, I sealed my lips around him and sucked. By now, his cock was rock hard and big enough that I knew I'd never get it all in my mouth.

Massaging his balls in one hand, I used the other, together with my mouth, as I started to work the length of his shaft. I stopped at the top and swirled my tongue around the swollen head, enjoying the taste of his excitement.

It was too much for Grant, and with a low growl, his hands tightened on my head again, covering my ears, and he started to thrust upward. I brought my hands back, using them to brace myself on his knees as he held me close and fucked my mouth. The pounding of my heart echoed through my body as my husband's scent filled my head. I moaned at the pure joy of serving him and welcomed it when he pulled me tight against him again and spilled his seed down my throat.

His grip loosened and I pulled back a bit. After sucking in a bit of air, I bent forward again and licked at his softening cock, cleaning him.

It was then that I realized that my own arousal had taken on less urgency. It was still there, a low, level hum alive in my body, but it was dwarfed by the pleasure of satisfying my man.

"Thank you, baby." Grant stroked a hand lovingly over my head once, then lifted his hips and pulled his shorts back up. "You can go eat your dinner now."

Realizing I was dismissed, I climbed to my feet and started to leave the room. When I was at the door, Grant's voice stopped me.

"Bethany."

"Yes?" I turned toward him.

"You are not to masturbate or touch yourself, at all, until I tell you." His gaze was steady, watchful, as he spoke.

Chapter Fifteen

Sunday was okay, Monday was hell.

"Are you going to sulk all day or are you going to tell me what's going on?" Ginger had been quiet all day and that meant something was wrong. By three o'clock I'd had enough.

"Nothing is going on," she said as she waved good-bye to her customer.

I reached for the hand she'd rested on the counter and clasped it between mine. "Ginger, I've known you for far too long for that to work. I know when you're this quiet, something is wrong. Please tell me, sweetie."

"I'll tell you mine, if you'll tell me yours." Her troubled brown eyes met mine and I thought about it.

She knew about my brushes with exhibitionism, and she knew

that Grant and I were still together, but that was it. In fact, that was all that I knew too. It had occurred to me that morning that, although Grant hadn't left me or thrown a fit, we hadn't made up. Not really.

Then again, we hadn't really had a fight either.

I was confused, and the offer to spill my guts to Ginger was very appealing. But first I had to find out what was bothering her. "Deal."

"It's nothing major," she said with a shrug. "It's just that Jason hasn't called me again."

"It has only been a couple of days, Ginger."

"I know. I'm just not used to waiting for a man to call. Normally, if they don't call, it's because they already got what they wanted from me. But Jason didn't get anything more than a kiss." She folded her arms across her chest. "He didn't want anything more than a kiss."

I couldn't help it. A laugh bubbled up in my throat and I coughed madly trying to keep it from bursting forth.

"Beth! It's not funny."

"I'm sorry," I tried to hide my grin at her hurt look. "But your worrying over a man wanting nothing more than kiss, when only last week you were upset because the only thing men wanted from you was sex, struck me as funny."

Her cheeks turned pink and a giggle escaped. "I know! It's Jason. It's so strange. We had coffee once, and a couple of games of pool and I can't get him out of my mind."

"You know why, don't you?"

"Why?"

"Because you *like* him."

"What's that supposed to mean?"

"It means that you just might be starting a real relationship here. That you're actually getting to know him before inviting him into your bed, and it's going to pay off for you."

Something akin to fear flashed across her face and she grimaced at me. "I umm, I actually already invited him into my bed."

"Ginger!"

Pink-cheeked, she gave me a small smile and her words came tumbling out. "It was Friday night, and we'd had a great time at Smiley's, and when he kissed me good night and I felt how hard his body was, and I remembered you saying he had his nipples pierced, I just couldn't stop myself. Only he said no."

"That's a good thing, Ginger."

"I sort of thought so too, but it's been a couple days now, and I still haven't heard from him, so I'm not so sure anymore. Maybe I was too aggressive, and it turned him off."

"If it did, then it's okay. You're aggressive in everything you do, Ginger, and you shouldn't change that for any man. If it's a turnoff for him, then he isn't the one for you."

"I guess so."

She looked so down that I pulled her to me in a hug. "It's all right, sweetie. It might just be that he's super busy at work. The ad campaign he and Grant have been working on is supposed to be pitched to the client either today or tomorrow. God knows it's kept Grant busy."

"Yeah? I thought things were better after the whole exhibition thing? That he was going to spend more time with you?"

I glanced over Ginger's shoulder at the girl who'd just walked into the store. She was in her early teens, not our usual clientele. "Just a sec," I whispered to Ginger.

It was wrong of me to assume she was going to try to shoplift, but after so many years in the business I trusted my instincts. I walked out from behind the sales counter and greeted the customer. Sure enough, as soon as I said hello, she turned and exited the store.

Ginger and I shared a look before she started in on me.

"C'mon Beth, what's going on in the Mack household?"

Part of me really wanted to tell her everything, but the new dynamic, the new feelings and emotions and sexual power exchange was . . . well, it was new.

And very private.

"It was just a bit weird last weekend."

"Good weird? Bad weird? C'mon woman, give me the down and dirty."

I shook my head a little. "There are no down and dirty details. He came home on Friday and told me not to do it again. When I explained why I'd done it in the first place, that I was feeling a little unattractive and forgotten, he, umm, proved to me that I was always attractive to him."

Heat crept up my neck, and I knew I was blushing.

She arched an eyebrow at me. "Then what's the problem? And don't tell me nothing, because I don't like to be lied to."

"To be honest, Ginger, I don't know what the problem is." A self-conscious laugh escaped. "If you'd asked me last week, I'd have said it was something silly like the spark was gone, or I was lonely because I wasn't getting enough sex. But, well, that's not a problem anymore."

Except that yesterday, instead of spending Sunday afternoon running errands with me, or watching a movie with me like he used to, Grant worked. Sure, he worked at home, and when I went into his office to greet him *properly*, he gave me such a sizzling kiss, my knees were weak and my pussy was damp before he sent me out of the room.

"Hmm."

I came back to earth to see Ginger smirking at me. "What?"

"You're hungover."

"Excuse me?"

She laughed at me. "You're suffering from withdrawal of cock. Let me guess, you and Grant weren't doing it for a while, then on Friday you had makeup sex, which continued into the weekend, and now, it's Monday afternoon, and you wish you were home in bed with your husband. You're in withdrawal."

I caught a movement out of the corner of my eye, and I turned. A new customer. Ginger patted me on the shoulder and went to greet her, leaving me to wonder if she was right.

Damn it, I think she was. Not only did I only get a kiss after such intense experiences the previous day or two, but I hadn't masturbated since Friday. It was only three days, but that was two days longer than I had let go by in months.

Grant had told me not to pleasure myself, and I automatically listened. Which worked fine when he was there to keep me in line . . . but what was stopping me from doing it now?

My lips curved into a grin and the wicked pull of being naughty sparked a fire low in my belly.

Chapter Sixteen

When I got home from work on Monday night, Grant was sound asleep on the sofa. Before I slid the file from under his hands and set it on the table, I took a moment to just look at him. My husband.

The man I loved with all my heart.

In that moment, my plans to masturbate if he didn't make love to me that night went straight out the window. When I looked at him, everything else faded away and nothing mattered but making him happy. Putting on those little teaser shows for other men had been so wrong. It didn't matter that Ginger was right, that I hadn't physically cheated, but I *had* betrayed a certain trust. And I wasn't going to do it again by disobeying a direct order. Even if Grant never found out, I would know, and that was enough.

"I'm home." I leaned down and whispered the words against his lips.

His eyes opened slowly, and he gave me a soft smile.

"Let's get you to bed, baby. Sleeping here will give you nothing but a stiff neck and a headache."

A drowsy Grant wrapped his arm around my shoulders and, hips bumping, we went up the stairs and climbed into bed together.

I woke up super early the next morning. It was still dark out, and the neon orange numbers on the bedside clock told me Grant would wake up and go to work soon. For a while, I just lay there next to him, listening to his smooth, even breathing, drinking in the sight of him, soft and gentle in sleep.

He took my breath away.

The magic of him being in my bed next to me, the security of knowing I was his, and he was mine, was more intoxicating than any flirtation or tease could be.

My fingers itched to run through his thick hair, to cup his cheek and feel the stubble of his morning beard against the palm of my hand. The need to touch him, to assure myself that he was there, that it was real and not just a dream was strong.

So strong that I couldn't resist.

Inching my way across the sheet, I touched the palm of his hand and watched his fingers twitch. I trailed my fingers lightly up his arm, lingering over the rounded bicep and the curve of his shoulder. I scraped my nail against the stubble on his cheek and watched as he blinked awake.

"Good morning," I whispered.

"Good morning," he whispered back.

He reached out, wrapped an arm around my waist, and pulled me tightly to him. The large male hand traveled over my hip and down my thigh to my knee. With one slow, sure movement he pulled my leg over his and slid inside me.

We didn't speak; no words were needed.

We stared into each other's eyes, breathed each other's air, and moved our hips in a well-synchronized dance. Grant picked up speed just a little, and I watched as his eyes darkened and his brow furrowed. His hand squeezed my buttock, then slipped lower, his finger finding the little puckered hole there. He pressed gently against it and my insides spasmed, pleasure rolling up and out from my core to warm my whole body. It wasn't a big orgasm, but as I watched Grant's face tighten and felt his cock jerk and twitch as he came, it was okay. I'd pleased him, and that gave me pleasure.

Chapter Seventeen

Even though the day started out great, it soon went to shit for me. Grant's proposal date got pushed back to Thursday, and he wasn't happy about it. I figured a couple extra days to get everything polished and perfect would be a good thing, but obviously I knew nothing about advertising. He said the proposal was perfect as it was, but if he had to sit on it for a couple of days he might not be able to keep from messing with it some more.

Tuesday night I'd been hoping for some loving attention. The morning sex had been a nice wake-up, but it had only whet my appetite for more. Unfortunately, I was still determined to obey Grant's edict of no masturbating, and he was so tense on Tuesday night that any type of lovin' was not an option.

Wednesday morning, I rolled over in bed while Grant was getting dressed. I wanted to ask him to come back to bed, to let me put us both in a better mood with a proper wake-up. But there was such an angry cloud hanging over him that I couldn't squeeze the words past my throat. Instead, I asked if he wanted to spend the evening watching movies with me.

"I can see if I can get Samair to close the shop tonight, and I'll pick them up on the way home. . . ."

"Sure. It might help keep my mind off the project for a bit." He gave me a tight smile and left for work.

Curled up together on the sofa used to be our favorite way of just hanging out together. It had been our Sunday evening thing, but it had slacked off when Grant's workload got too heavy. Now that the project was completed, I hoped to get things back to normal. Somewhat.

The day was slow, and Samair had been eager for the extra hours, so by late afternoon, I was in my car heading away from work. I went grocery shopping, and just as I was pulling up in front of the video store, my cell phone rang. The caller i.d. showed our home number so I answered it.

"Are you at the video store yet?" Grant asked.

"Just drove up. Was there something specific you wanted to see?" I liked the sound of that. It meant he'd actually thought about our plans.

"Yes, there is. I called ahead and they have them on hold at the desk so you just have to pick them up."

"Sounds great. I already got the groceries and a six-pack of beer for you. Did you want anything else while I'm out?"

"No, that's it. And Bethany?"

"Yes?"

"The movies are a surprise so don't ask him what they are, and don't peek."

That firm command made my insides quiver, and, suddenly, the sun was brighter and the day much, much better. "Yes, sir. I'll be home as soon as I'm done here."

Curiosity over what movies Grant had requested worked in tandem with the knowledge that he was going to spend the evening with me. When I got home, I went straight to Grant's office and stood at his side until he stopped what he was doing and turned to me. When I leaned down to give him a kiss hello, his hand squeezed the back of my neck and he ravished my mouth. His tongue invaded, his teeth nipped at my lips, and his flavor filled me. When he let me go, he gave me a devilish grin and turned back to his work without a word.

Floating a few inches off the ground, I went into the kitchen to make dinner. When the salad was tossed and the chicken breasts cooked, I went to peek in at Grant.

"Ready for dinner and a movie?"

He sat back in his chair and scrubbed a hand roughly over his face. "Give me five more minutes?"

He was asking me? "Of course."

Exactly five minutes later, he strode into the kitchen and exclaimed how hungry he was. "Let's pop a movie in and watch in the living room."

Grant picked up the wrapped videos (I'd never seen them wrap videos before, obviously Grant had told the clerk they were supposed to be a surprise) and went into the living room. I followed him a minute later with the food on plates and joined him on the sofa.

When the movie screen came up, I saw that it was just a big dumb action movie. Not my favorite thing, but one I could live with. I shot him a quizzical look, but he ignored it, leaving me to wonder why he'd wanted it to be a surprise.

After eating, we settled back on the sofa, side by side, and watched. About halfway though the movie, during the obligatory sex scene after the hero saved the damsel in distress, I realized that Grant and I weren't talking.

We hadn't really talked in a while. Not since I'd told him what I'd done. There were "good mornings" and "good nights," and a few basic sentences throughout the day but that was it. The only time Grant really spoke to me was when we were having sex. When he was giving me commands.

There was no denying that the new direction our love life had taken was exciting. But in gaining the new direction, I couldn't help but wonder if I was losing something too.

"Ready for the next one?"

"Huh?" Startled out of my thoughts I glanced at the television where the credits were rolling. "Oh yeah, of course. You want me to put it in?"

"Why don't you grab me another beer, and I'll put it in."

It wasn't a question. It was a reminder that he'd picked out the movies, and since the first one was no big surprise, I knew this one would be. My pulse sped up just a bit while I went to the kitchen. I dropped off our dinner plates and grabbed him another beer. When I returned to the living room, Grant was seated in the big club chair, remote control in hand, wicked gleam in his eyes.

I handed him his beer and sank down onto the sofa. Then I

looked at the screen and saw an old film start. A classic? He'd wanted me to rent some black-and-white classic?

As I watched, I realized it wasn't really black-and-white, just sort of a faded color, and dreamy-looking. When the title came up, my breath caught in my throat.

The Story of O.

Chapter Eighteen

'd heard of the book, but never read it. Erotica was never really my thing. But as the movie played, and I realized what the story was actually about—domination and belonging to someone—my opinion changed.

The story might be just the one for me to read. I tried to pay attention to the movie, but soon my body distracted me. My breasts grew heavy, the nipples tight. My pulse seemed centered between my legs, each heartbeat a throb of awareness. Grant and I had watched porn together once or twice in the first year after our wedding, and each time, it had been Grant's reaction to the screen happenings that had turned me on. Not the actual antics I'd seen.

This time was different though. This time I watched carefully, wishing that the movie wasn't so old, that maybe it was a little less erotica and more pornographic.

Every time I tore my gaze from the screen to glance at Grant, he was watching me. I wanted to go to him, to climb onto his lap, or to get on my knees in front of him. I wanted to hear him call me his and make me feel that it was true. But I didn't go to him, and he didn't call to me.

Instead, the room remained silent except for the movie.

When the final credits of the movie rolled, I stayed exactly as I was while Grant turned the television and lights off. I was strangely frozen, unsure of myself. Unsure of what the movie choice meant and of what would happen next. The only thing I knew for certain was that whatever it was, it was up to Grant.

My gaze followed him as he set the DVD cases on the coffee table and started from the room. He stopped at the doorway and turned back to me. "Coming?"

I jumped from the sofa and followed him up the stairs to the bedroom. "On the bed," he ordered as he started to undress.

With a few quick movements, I was rid of my own clothes and stretched out naked on the bed before my husband. I waited with bated breath for him to give me another order, or position me for his pleasure. Instead, he stood next to the bed, and began to stroke his jutting erection.

"Did the movie turn you on?" he asked.

"Oh, yes," I replied.

"Yes, what?"

My heart kicked and my pussy clenched. "Yes, sir."

"Did you want to be her? Did you want to be used and trained?"

I hesitated, eyes glued to the way his hand played with only the tip of his cock. He was teasing himself.

"Bethany?"

The warning note in his tone brought me back to the question. Did I want to be O? Heat crawled up my neck. "No, I didn't want to be her. Not really."

"Why not?" His rhythm changed, his strokes becoming longer as he pulled at his entire length. "Beth!"

My eyes snapped up to his. "What?"

"Did I say you could touch yourself?"

One of my hands had crept over my belly and breast. I'd been about to pinch my nipple when the harsh command had stopped my unconscious wandering. "No, sir. I'm sorry, sir."

I squeezed my thighs together and hoped he wouldn't stop. I'd never seen him pleasure himself before. I'd seen him give it a tug or two, but never actually masturbate. Now I knew why men found it so arousing to watch me. It was incredibly erotic.

"I was going to let you suck my cock, but you haven't earned it. First you ignored my question, and then you try to play with yourself. I told you the other day. You aren't to do that unless I say so. Now you'll just have to watch. No touching yourself, or me."

Despair rolled over me and a whimper escaped. Grant's lips twisted in a mocking smile, and he stepped closer. Close enough that I could smell his arousal, that I could see every vein, and every twitch of his cock.

No touching!

Another whimper escaped, and I begged him with my eyes. The sight of his fingers wrapped around his cock, his hand pumping up and down his length was almost enough in itself to make me come. I knew it would only take a little touch. I rubbed my thighs together, squeezing my inner muscles and was rewarded with a small wave of pleasure. A hint of an orgasm. I was so close.

"You need to answer my question, Bethany."

I searched my mind, digging through the sexual fog to try to remember the question.

"Answer me quickly, before I come, and I *might* let you masturbate tomorrow." The head of his cock had turned a deep purple, shiny with the start of his own orgasm. My mouth watered and I licked my lips.

Answer his question . . . what question? His hand pumped faster, his abs flexed and his thighs bulged . . . he was going to come . . . why . . . he'd asked me why I hadn't wanted to be her . . . the woman in the movie . . . O.

"Because I only want to be trained by you, to be used by you." The words leapt from my lips, mingling with his grunt of satisfaction as come shot from his cock and landed hot on my breasts.

Seconds later Grant braced his knees on the edge of the bed and used one hand to rub his juices into my skin. "You are mine, and only mine. I will train you, and I will use you."

I knew I should want to go wash off, but I didn't. Instead, when Grant pulled back the sheet and collapsed on the bed, I curled up next to him, my lack of orgasm forgotten in the pleasure of having his scent all over me. The pleasure of knowing I was only his.

Chapter Nineteen

"**A**re you alone?"

"Sort of," I replied into the phone.

I glanced around the shop. Ginger was in the changing area with a customer, but other than that the place was empty.

"Sort of isn't good enough, Bethany. Are you or are you not alone?" Grant's voice deepened.

My pulse picked up and the sting of loneliness I'd had when I'd woken up alone that morning dissipated. "Ginger's with a customer in the dressing area, but that's it."

"Can she watch the store while you take a break? I need you."

. . .

parked in the lot of Grant's advertising firm and headed inside the building. My heart was pounding, and my mind was racing.

After such intense erotic encounters over the weekend, and the disconcerting lack of sexual contact at the start of the week, I'd been feeling just a little bit lost. Then there was the night before: the movie and masturbation show. To say I was off-kilter would be putting it mildly, and to top it all off, I'd been anxiously fighting the urge to diddle myself in the ladies' room at work all morning. Grant's call had been a welcome distraction, his invitation undeniable.

With sure steps that didn't show how wobbly my knees were, I strode across the lobby and up the stairs to the second-floor offices. Grant's secretary was on the phone, but she waved me past when she saw me and I entered his office.

"Hi baby," I greeted him.

"Close the door," Grant said without looking up from his papers.

After shutting it softly, I went over to one of the large padded chairs in front of his desk and sank down. I sat quietly, hands in my lap and waited. Pulse pounding and insides trembling, my body readied itself for whatever Grant needed.

He kept working, so to distract myself I glanced around his office. It wasn't my first time there, but it still surprised me how luxurious it was. Two padded leather visitor chairs, a large, sturdy desk made from some rich-looking wood, bookshelves lining one wall, and various ad paraphernalia on the other.

"Done," Grant said with a finality that had my head snapping back to him.

A wicked gleam brightened his eyes as he leaned back in his chair and looked me over. "Another dress, hmm? Do you have panties on under it this time?"

Swallowing nervously, I shook my head.

"Good." He waved at the portfolio on his desk. "My presentation is in an hour, and I need a distraction or I'm just going to keep fiddling with it, and since it's perfect as it is, that wouldn't be a good idea. So I figured it was time for you to do for me what you were so eager to do for a few strangers."

Before I had time to figure out exactly how to take that comment, he spoke again. "Show me what you do, Bethany. Show me how you get off."

A thrill shot through me. I straightened in my chair and glanced at the closed, but unlocked door. "Here?"

"Here." His voice was firm. "Now."

Then, suddenly, I was unsure. I lifted trembling fingers to my face and pushed back a lock of hair. "Umm, What do you want me to do? How do you want me to start?"

"I want you to make yourself come, just for me, here and now. And know that you only have ten minutes to do it. If you can't make yourself come in ten minutes, then you won't get to come for . . . ten more hours."

It was just after eleven in the morning. If Grant made me wait until after nine that night, he'd be asleep and I'd be out of luck! What a devious form of torture!

"Nine minutes."

Sinking back into the chair I reached up and cupped a breast. Letting my eyes drift closed I pinched my nipple and ran my other hand up and down my bare thigh, lifting my skirt a bit more each time.

"Open your eyes, Bethany. I want you to know who you're performing for."

For some reason, watching Grant watch me was hard. My mind

balked at the idea, but my body loved it. My sex clenched and juices flowed south.

"Seven minutes."

Unable to stop myself, I glanced over my shoulder at the closed office door only to have Grant chuckle. "Don't worry, no one will come in without knocking first."

With an effort, I locked my gaze on Grant and went to work. Abandoning my breast, I slid the skirt of my dress up and swiped a finger across my swollen pussy lips. Holding my breath, I spread my legs wider and focused on the hard nub of nerves there.

The fire in Grant's eyes burned brighter as he watched me. What surprised me the most was that he didn't watch my fingers, he watched my face. His chest lifted and lowered in a smooth, if fast, rhythm, and I sucked my bottom lip between my teeth in an effort to control my own breathing.

His gaze flicked to my groin. "Five minutes."

The knot of pleasure in my lower belly tightened, and my hips pushed forward, pressing against my hand. I was close, so close. I'd been aching for an orgasm for days. It shouldn't have taken me more than two or three minutes at the most. But suddenly I didn't know if five would be enough.

And if I didn't come soon, I'd have to wait again.

Panic started to build in my chest, and I rubbed faster, harder. I reached lower and spread my slickness around some more, coating my clit, before rubbing again.

"Three minutes, Bethany."

My eyes started to drift closed, but I snapped them open. I ran my eyes over my husband, sitting back in his chair enjoying the show. There was an obvious tent in his trousers, but he made no move to touch himself. If only he would give himself a little rub, I knew it would send me over the edge.

"Two minutes."

My whole body was tight, tensed for a release that was so close, yet so far away. I was panting and straining for it. My thighs spread so wide they pressed against the edges of the chair. People walked by the door, phones rang, and yet, Grant and I were locked in our own erotic bubble.

"One minute."

A growl of frustration rumbled out of my throat. There . . . there . . . I felt it, the start of an orgasm. My eyes widened and my lips parted, Grant's cheeks flushed and he leaned forward as he saw what was happening. "That's it, baby. Come for me, Bethany."

A sharp rap on the door echoed loudly through the room just as I slipped over the edge. I snapped my legs together, trapping my hand there as shockwaves of pleasure rolled through me. My eyes closed, and I bit down on my lip to stay silent as the door to the office opened behind me, and my whole world became the sensations that reverberated through me.

When I came back to myself, Grant was looking over my shoulder. "I'll be there in five minutes, Margaret. Thank you."

The door clicked shut behind me, and I started to shake, tears welling in my eyes. Grant moved swiftly as he came around the desk and pulled me out of the chair by my shoulders.

"Shhh, it's okay, baby." He cradled me against his chest and tucked my head beneath his chin. My skirt fell back around my legs as I slipped my hands around his waist. "You did great. Margaret didn't see a thing. She just stuck her head in and your back was to her anyway. It's all good, baby. You did good."

His crooning words were so comforting, and I felt so safe and secure in his arms. I pressed closer and his hard-on nudged my belly. With a soft mewl of distress I slid my hand from his back to reach between our bodies.

Grant caught my hand before I reached his cock and shushed me. "It's okay, baby. Just relax."

I pushed against his chest and looked up into his face, my words soft and beseeching, "But I want to please you."

"You did please me."

"But you didn't come."

He shook his head. "I know you want me to come, but all I wanted was to watch you. And right now, what I want is what matters, right?"

I nodded, disappointed that I wouldn't get to touch him.

He set me back from him a bit and clasped my hands in his. "I have to go to my lunch meeting, now. You go back to work and I'll see you at home tonight, okay?"

I nodded, still feeling all soft and warm, the longing to remain close to him becoming a natural part of me.

"You did great, Bethany. You've earned a big reward for later tonight." He kissed me softly then spun me around and patted me on the butt. "Now get back to work."

During the quick drive back to the shop, I marveled at how our sex life had changed in less than a week. Grant had surprised me—hell, I'd surprised myself—and I knew there was even more to come. For the rest of the day, my body hummed in anticipation as I wondered what my "big reward" might be.

Chapter Twenty

By the time I pulled into the driveway at home I was strung tight again. Anticipation was a good thing, but too much of it was turning out to be torture.

I swung open the front door and strode inside. Before I could open my mouth and call out a greeting, Grant was in the foyer. Beer in hand, grin in place, he swept me up in his arms and danced around. "Go get changed, we have a late dinner reservation at nine thirty."

"That's in less than fifteen minutes, Grant!"

He let me go. "You better hurry then."

That was the playful, yet commanding man I'd known before we got married. I spun around and dashed up the stairs. Panic and excitement mixed as they ran through my veins. Dinner reservations? And Grant dressed casually in jeans and button-up shirt, so not a business dinner.

A date! Grant and I were going on a date.

God, I couldn't remember the last time we'd had a date!

I raced into the bathroom and pulled my sundress over my head. Dropping it on the floor, I did a quick body wash with a wet cloth, before dashing naked into the bedroom and coming to a dead stop. Laid out on the bed was my little black dress. The one I only wear on special occasions, not because it's so fancy, but because it makes me feel so completely special.

With slow steps, I walked over to the bed and picked up the dress. The soft rayon blend was filmy and sexy in my hands. The sound of footsteps and a tingle at the back of my neck told me Grant was behind me. I turned slowly, dress in hands.

He was leaning against the doorway, eyes intent as he watched me.

I raised an eyebrow in question and he nodded. With a naughty smile and a sense of playfulness, I lifted the dress over my head and was about to let it fall when he spoke from his position in the doorway.

"Take off your bra first."

Our eyes met. He'd never picked out my clothes before, or tried to tell me how to dress, but there was no room for argument in that gaze. The anticipation that had me strung so tight earlier returned full force, only this time it centered itself as a knot of arousal low in my belly.

In one quick movement, I had my bra off, then I scooped up my dress again and slipped it over my head. A simple tank-style dress, it hit my shoulders and skimmed over my curves. My nipples beaded as the heavy material rubbed against them gently. The weight of it gave the dress sway as it clung in all the right places, making it flirty and sexy.

Making me feel flirty and sexy.

I went to the dresser and pulled out a pair of black lace French-cut panties. Before I could attempt to step into them Grant cleared his throat. "You like going without panties, so none of those either."

"But this skirt is a lot shorter than my sundresses." I stared at him. "If I bend over to fix my shoe or don't sit perfectly, I'll flash everyone!"

His lips twisted. "No panties."

Ooh!

The knot in my gut tightened just a little.

I tried not to let my grin get too big as I turned back to the dresser and started to brush my hair.

"Pin it up."

I glanced at Grant's reflection in the mirror and did as he asked. My breasts swayed and Grant's gaze followed them as I twisted my hair up and jammed a couple of pins into place. This date was going to be different from any we'd ever been on. I could feel it. My pussy was already slick again, and I was praying I'd make it through dinner without begging him to take me home and fuck me hard.

Not that I hadn't felt that turned on when on a date with my husband before, but Grant's flirty playfulness was gone, and in its place was the quiet strength and confidence of the new masterful man I was still getting to know.

The urge to please, to submit to only him, was strong within me. But so was the naughty streak that my exhibitionist experiences had given birth to.

Maybe we could be just a little late for dinner?

I leaned over the dresser in the guise of applying some lipstick, and arched my back in a way that I knew he'd see everything I had to offer. He pushed off from the doorway and entered the room. My heart pounded as he got closer, the flames of desire leaping in his eyes.

"You are such a little tease," he said when he was next to me. A warm hand slid under my skirt and between my thighs. He cupped my sex and a long finger dipped into the slick heat to tease me for just a moment before he pulled back. Then the flat of his hand came down sharply on my bare ass. Once, twice, three times in quick succession. "That was just a reminder of the last time you flashed someone like that. Now stand up straight."

I tried to get control of my breathing as the heat from my rear drew all my focus between my legs. Grant set his empty beer bottle on the dresser and pulled something from the second drawer. In one smooth move he was behind me. I watched in the mirror as he drew a thin black velvet corded choker around my neck.

I fingered the little silver ring that sat at the center of my neck while he did the clasp at the back. It was very pretty, and a bit unusual.

Grant smiled over my shoulder. "This is a collar, *your collar*. It means you belong to me. Understand?"

I nodded.

He reached a hand around and pinched a pebbled nipple through my dress, making me gasp. "I said . . . understand?"

"Yes, sir."

"Good. Let's go."

He turned and I followed him from the room.

Grant parked at the curb a few cars away from the door of the Irish restaurant-style pub. I'd heard about Shaunessey's but had never been there before, so I was pleasantly surprised when we walked in to find it had a bit of the pub atmosphere, with a small stage for a band and a dance floor. The bar was in the middle of the room, and the four surrounding walls were lined with padded booths, separated by high dark wood dividers, so each one was semiprivate.

Grant held my hand and led the way to the back of the room. As I walked, I was highly aware of my pantyless state. The skirt swayed and if I walked too fast, anyone looking might get a flash of my bare ass. I wondered if my butt cheeks were still pink from the couple of swats Grant had given me. Probably not.

When Grant stopped in front of a table, I was surprised that two people were already seated there. Ginger and Jason.

"Hey, guys," I said as casually as possible. I tried to curb my disappointment at not having Grant all to myself. After all, I had been the one who wanted to see Ginger and Jason get together.

I slid into the booth, careful to tuck my dress underneath me, and Grant slid in next to me, close enough that the denim of his jeans brushed teasingly against my bare skin with every movement.

"Isn't it great, Beth?" Ginger asked.

"Umm, what?" Did I miss something? My mind was so focused on my body that I'd clearly missed part of the conversation.

"About the Red's Project. The guys hit it out of the park!"

Grant put his arm around my shoulder and pulled me close. He leaned down and nuzzled my ear then whispered, "After your invigorating visit to the office this afternoon, our presentation went off without a hitch, and we landed the account. When we were leaving the office, Jason mentioned he was seeing Ginger tonight, so I figured we could all celebrate together."

Together? All of us? Celebrate?

I bent my head close to Grant's. "Is this the big reward you promised me?"

He threw back his head and laughed. "No, baby. That's just for you . . . later. This is just dinner."

Jason and Ginger gave us funny looks but didn't say anything. The waiter arrived to ask what we'd like to drink, and we decided to order dinner right away too.

"And for you, beautiful lady?" The young waiter turned his charming smile on me.

Heat bloomed in my cheeks at the twinkle in his chocolate-brown puppy-dog eyes. He was flirting with me!

Pleasure bubbled up inside of me and I smiled at him. "I'll have the shepherd's pie, please."

"Will that be everything for you?"

Grant's hand twitched on my shoulder. It was a normal question, one that servers ask all the time. But the inflection in his voice had all sorts of requests popping into my dirty mind. The heat in my cheeks intensified. "Yes, that's everything for now, thank you."

Both men ordered steaks, of course, and with a last quick glance my way, the waiter left.

Conversation centered on food in general, the pub (none of us had been there before), and the success of their pitch that day. Wine flowed steadily for Ginger and me while the men nursed their beers. When the food arrived, Grant pulled his arm from around me so he could eat, and the loss of his touch made my heart ache.

"Don't be silly," I told myself. "He's right next to you. You don't have to be touching constantly."

Yet, the ache remained.

Chapter Twenty-one

What do you think of the size of your man's meat there, Bethany?" Jason asked with a playful smirk.

I pasted a serene expression on my face and replied in complete seriousness. "Sometimes I think it's too big, but he knows what he's doing, so all's well."

"Bethany!" Ginger cried.

Grant patted my thigh, and Jason gave me a mock salute before cutting into his own steak.

"I've always said a talented man is much better than a large one," Ginger said with a wicked smile aimed at Jason. "Second only to an adventurous one."

Jason's reply was lost to me when Grant's hand slipped under the table and up my leg. I sat back against the booth and glanced over at him. He laughed at whatever Jason had said, not looking my way.

But his fingers kept tracing patterns on the inside of my thigh and his hand continued to creep up my leg. He stopped a millimeter away from my swollen pussy lips.

His touch was so close. I reached for my wineglass with a shaky hand and took a much needed sip. Just as I was about to set it back on the table, he nudged my clit and I dropped my glass with a gasp.

"Graceful, Bethany." Ginger gave me a speculative look. My best friend knew it was rare for me to fumble or drop anything.

Jason waved the waiter over and I tried to soak up the spilled liquid with my napkin. Which left my lap open to the view of the waiter, with Grant's hand still high up on my bare thigh. The waiter removed my empty dinner plate and mopped up the table in front of me with a knowing grin.

"Not a problem at all," he said when I'd thanked him. "I'm sure you were enjoying *it* before the spill. Would you like another?"

Another rub of my clit? Another glass of wine?

"Yes, please." I met his laughing gaze and smiled confidently. "Another would be wonderful."

So he saw Grant's hand in my lap and guessed we were playing around a bit. Not a big deal. It's not like I hadn't done more than that in front of a stranger before. However, I'd not done it with Grant, or with my best friend and her date across from us.

The waiter left and conversation resumed. I leaned into Grant's side and placed my hand on *his* thigh, earning a small smile.

My wine arrived, and the rest of the dinner plates were cleared, but Grant's hand stayed in one spot with no wandering fingers. I wiggled deeper into my seat. Nothing. I leaned forward and rested my elbows on the table. Nothing.

Except when I leaned forward, my nipples brushed against the edge of the table. I crossed my arms, one hand hiding behind the other arm, and managed to tweak my own nipple while everyone talked and laughed. No one knew what I was up to.

That's what I thought, until Grant squeezed my thigh and gave his head a small shake. I smiled at him, and inched my legs farther apart. When Grant responded by skimming his fingers over my sex, I thought I'd finally gotten what I'd wanted. Only, he just teased.

He brushed across my sex, dipped into my slit, and nudged my entrance. Not once did he focus his touch on my clit. I knew if he did, it would only take seconds for the knot of pleasure in my belly to explode. I'd been on the edge for so long, I completely lost track of the conversation as I tried inching forward on my seat. The instant I moved, Grant's hand froze, then he withdrew it.

I couldn't take any more.

I nudged Grant. "I need to go to the ladies' room, please. Sir."

My tone of voice was playful, but calling him "sir" made Grant's eye flare, making me feel powerful. He slid out of the booth and helped me to do the same.

"Wait for me." Ginger ushered Jason out of his side of the booth.

"Do *not* make yourself come," Grant whispered in my ear while I waited for Ginger to stand up. "I'll know if you do."

His gaze was hot when I met it. Arousal and confidence glowed from deep within him. I nodded, acknowledging his command.

"Okay, let's go," Ginger held out a hand to me.

The two of us headed toward the back of the pub. Ginger's strides were long, and my breasts bounced and my skirt swayed with every step as I tried to keep up. The heat of strangers' eyes on me as I walked made my skin tingle and all my blood rush to my core.

We didn't talk until we entered the washroom. "Woo-hoo, Bethany. Look at you go, girlfriend!"

"What are you talking about?" I laughed and entered the stall quickly. God, I wanted to frig myself so much!

"You are *hot*."

She was telling me? My insides were on fire and I was alone in a bathroom stall, unable to relieve myself. "You've seen me in this dress before," I called out as casually as I could.

After cleaning myself up a little, I flushed the toilet and drowned out Ginger's next words.

When she joined me at the sink she smirked. "It's not just the dress. You are glowing and everyone can see it. Every eye in the house was on you when we walked back here."

Color flooded my cheeks. I'd tried to walk steadily so nobody would catch a peek under my skirt. Really, I had.

"It wasn't me they were staring at, honey, it was you. You're just immune to the looks because you get them so much."

"No." Ginger shook her head and smiled gently. "It was you, and I'm okay with that. I'm happy for you, babe. You look like you're falling in love all over again."

I held out my hand for her lip gloss. "Grant and I are doing really well."

"So I see." She glanced pointedly at my collar.

"What?" I tried to look innocent.

"The collar explains a lot."

"Collar?" I raised a hand and fingered the velvet-covered cord. "Isn't it pretty? It goes beautifully with this dress."

Fortunately, I went to Catholic school as a child and had the innocent look down pat. Ginger giggled and let it go. "Uh-huh."

"What about you?" I asked. "I told you Jason would call!"

She blushed. She actually blushed. "He didn't call me. I called him."

"You called him?" That was a first. I don't think Ginger had ever called a man.

"Yup."

I'd never seen Ginger with quite that expression on her face before. "Good for you. I just know you and Jason are going to be good together. And I expect you to remember I said this when you ask me to be your bridesmaid."

"Shut up!"

We left the washroom laughing and giggling.

Chapter Twenty-two

Our outing ended shortly after that. Grant gave me a warm grin when we returned to the table, and I was glad I'd fought the urge to play with myself. When we finished that round of drinks, Grant made our excuses and we got ready to leave.

I gave Ginger a wink when the men were saying good night. "I want details tomorrow," I whispered as I climbed out of the booth.

Grant led me from the restaurant with a guiding hand at the small of my back. He opened all the doors for me and helped me get seated in the car before shutting me in.

Gentleman that he is, he'd always done those things for me, and having him still do them that night took away some of the unease that had been growing inside me. The tender care made me feel very special and looked after.

Once we were in the car and on our way home, Grant kept both hands on the steering wheel.

My fingers curled until my nails bit into the palms. The little bit of self-induced pain kept me from sinking too far into the erotic fog that had been creeping over my mind ever since Grant had patted my pussy.

Soon, we were parked in our driveway, and Grant was opening the car door for me. He held out his hand, helped me from the car, and after interlocking his fingers with mine, led me into the house.

As soon as the door closed behind him I pressed myself against his body, and tried to kiss him. Grant didn't let go of my hand but instead, sidestepped me, and started up the stairs, pulling me behind him.

Once in the bedroom he let go of me, stepped back, and said one word.

"Present."

For a moment, I was completely blank. Then the image of myself on my knees and elbows that first night rushed to the forefront of my brain. Instantly, my need tripled.

Without a second thought, I started to bend my knees.

"On the bed," Grant ordered. "Take off the dress, but leave the shoes on."

His eyes gleaming like emeralds lit from within, Grant watched as I removed my dress in one swift motion and climbed onto the bed. Once in the center of the mattress, I turned so that he was behind me, and bent forward, bracing my weight on my elbows.

"Spread your knees wider."

Biting the inside of my cheek, I shuffled my knees apart some more. Cool air wafted over the heat of my hungry sex, carrying the musky scent of my own arousal to my nose.

"That's my girl. Don't move until I tell you to," Grant purred. He came closer to the bed and skimmed his fingertip down my spine.

I arched in reaction, and dropped my forehead against the comforter. The sharp edge of my arousal softened as his hands drifted everywhere. He cupped a breast, pinched a nipple, slapped my ass, and slid a finger along my aching slit.

My muscles started to tremble, a soft whimper escaped from me, and the knot of arousal low in my belly grew steadily.

"On your back." Grant's voice was strong, confident.

I quickly turned over and watched as he stripped off his shirt and shucked his jeans. When he was standing naked at the side of the bed, I reached out a hand, eager to touch his cock, only to have it slapped.

My gaze shot up to his, surprised.

"Did I say you could touch?" A black brow arched regally.

The knot coiled tighter and I licked my suddenly dry lips. "No, sir."

"Then don't touch."

He walked to the end of the bed, near my feet. "Lie on your back . . . Spread your hands and legs apart."

I quickly did as he asked, and watched as he went around the bed to my dresser. He opened the top drawer, dug in under the panties and bras and came out with my vibrator. My heart pounded, my breath caught.

"You didn't think I knew about this, did you?" He waggled the translucent pink gel cock in the air. "I've always known about it. In fact, I've been waiting for you to ask me to use it on you. But I'm not waiting anymore."

He twisted the plastic knob at the bottom and the cock jumped to life, the low hum of its vibrations music to my ears.

Grant placed a knee on the bed and leaned over me. He touched the vibrating tip to my stomach, and trailed it around my navel. His lips twisted into a wicked smile as he floated the toy lightly over my ribs and around my breasts. He touched it to the hard tips of my breasts and I sighed, my eyes drifting shut as pleasure worked its way into my veins and wrapped me in its cocoon.

Neither of us spoke again as Grant teased my body. I was in this weird sort of Zen state, where no thought existed, only feelings. Even when Grant moved the toy down my body, I stayed there. He skimmed the vibrator lightly over my swollen pussy lips before nudging it into my wetness. He slid it back and forth lengthwise along my slit, constantly touching me. The tight knot returned, but the urgency of it was gone. It was just there, growing steadily with every touch.

Soon my hips were rolling, synchronized with Grant's movements. The tip of the toy nudged my entrance with every swipe, and I started to pant. My cunt clenched, eager to be filled.

"Please." The plea slipped from my lips.

"Please, what?"

My fingers gripped at the comforter beneath me, my legs spread even wider as I dug my heels into the mattress and lifted my hips toward Grant. "Please fill me."

"Grab your knees," he ordered.

My eyes snapped open. I bent my knees, hooked my hands behind them and pulled them up toward me. I could see Grant, framed between my legs, his eyes gleaming and his face tight as he took in the sight before him.

He swiped the vibrator over my slit one more time, then slid it lower . . . until the head of the rubber cock nudged against my puckered anus. My body jerked and a loud moan jumped from my lips at the vibrations against such tender nerves. So naughty, so dirty . . . so *good*.

"I'll fill you up, baby. You'll be so full you'll never think of another man again," Grant said as he pressed slow and steady until the vibrator breached my rear entrance.

I tossed my head from side to side on the pillow. Not from the slight pain of the anal play or because I wanted him to stop, but because of his words. There'd been pain there. A hurt in his voice that I wanted desperately to soothe, but the physical need he'd fostered all night long had me in its grip, and I couldn't speak. I opened my mouth but only passion sounds emerged.

When the vibrator was firmly seated in my ass, Grant gave the knob on the bottom another twist and the vibrations intensified, making me jerk and moan.

Grant shifted on the bed and cock in hand, he positioned himself between my spread legs. "I'll fill you up good, baby." With one quick thrust he was in deep. His hands cupped my knees and he used them for leverage as he held my gaze and fucked me.

His hips pistoned and his cock pounded into me, hammering away at my pussy while the vibrator stretched my ass. The knot in my belly had spread until my entire body was tight, my orgasm building in every muscle, every nerve, every molecule of my body.

"Please," I panted not even aware of what I was saying. "Yes . . . No . . . Yes, Grant. Please . . . fill me . . . *love me* . . ."

His hands jumped from my knees to my hips, his grip tight and he held me still and thrust home deep and true.

"Yes!" he roared, his cock twitching as he emptied himself inside me.

In my mind, I felt his come spread through my body, releasing the pleasure that had been held tight in every inch of me. I reached up and dug my nails into his shoulders, pulling him closer and lifting my own body off the bed as everything inside me released.

I don't know how much later it was, but when I became aware of things again, tears were leaking slowly from my eyes and Grant was gently removing the vibrator. He crawled back up on the bed next to me and I reached out to touch his dear face, only to be stopped.

Grant kissed the palm of the hand he'd caught before I could touch him, stretched out on his side, and tucked me against his chest. "Get some sleep, babe."

Chapter Twenty-three

I woke up alone. Again.

It's not like waking up alone on a weekday is a big deal. Grant does go to work early, and *if* I wanted to, I could get up when he did. But, I still hated mornings. I hated waking up alone on this particular morning because Grant had fallen asleep before I could talk to him. And I needed to talk to him.

His words while he was fucking me, the pain and hurt in his voice, convinced me that I hadn't been imagining things. While Grant might want me to think we'd moved past my little exhibitionist adventures, we hadn't.

He hadn't.

We needed to talk about it because I was not willing to let this ruin us . . . and if I left it alone I was scared it just might.

. . .

Okay, spill the details." Ginger had looked ready to burst ever since I strode into the shop fifteen minutes late that morning, but it had been too busy for us to chat until then. Samair had arrived about half an hour ago and was now helping a lady in the fitting rooms, which gave Ginger and me a chance to catch up.

"He likes me!" She clasped her hands together in front of her chest like a teenybopper in a fifties movie. Only she wasn't being facetious. She truly was giddy.

"Of course he likes you. What's not to like?"

"No, Bethany." She practically *glowed*. "I mean he really likes me. When we left Shaunessey's last night we walked home. He held my hand the whole time and we talked. It was . . ."

I couldn't help it, a laugh bubbled up and I shook my head at her. "It was a date, Ginger. A real date, not just a hookup with some guy who wanted to get laid."

Her stunned expression faded into an almost serene one. "Yeah," she nodded. "It was a date."

Samair came out of the fitting room with her customer. They came up to the register and I rang up the purchases while Samair and Ginger stepped away to straighten up a display.

"That girl is amazing." The client pointed at Samair with her Montblanc pen before reaching for the credit slip on the counter. "She whipped out a couple of safety pins and made everything fit like a dream. You should do whatever you can to keep her here."

I smiled and said good-bye to the customer. Then I just stood there, watching Samair and Ginger as they giggled like schoolgirls.

Samair had a long-term boyfriend, and it looked like Ginger was on her way into a real relationship. Samair had such talent, and Ginger such energy, and both of them had good hearts. I was lucky to have them in my life. But would I be lucky enough to keep the man of my heart in my life, or had I already lost him?

Chapter Twenty-four

When I got home from work that night, Grant was asleep on the sofa. This time the television was on, and no papers covered his chest. He'd fallen asleep while relaxing, and that made me happy. I placed a light kiss on his cheek. "I'm home."

"Hey, baby." His lips twisted into a slow, gentle smile and warmth softened his eyes. Not heat, as in lust, but warmth. In that moment, he looked at me and all thoughts of troubles or problems melted away.

"I love you, Grant." The words flowed easily from me.

Grant's hand squeezed the back of my neck, and he pulled me to him for a long seductive kiss. When I came up for air, the warmth had turned to heat and my body responded. But, I felt dirty and sweaty after several hours in the storage room at the shop that night. "I need to take a shower. I'll meet you in the bedroom?"

He placed another soft kiss on my lips and then let me go with a nod. I dashed up the stairs and stripped off my clothes in the bathroom while I waited for the shower to hit the right temperature.

Maybe I was overreacting. Maybe Grant had just needed time, and everything was going to be all right again. We just needed to spend more time together as a couple. After I dried off I slathered lotion on my body and padded naked to the bedroom with heart pounding and blood humming.

And found Grant sound asleep, snoring contentedly.

By Saturday night, we still hadn't reconnected. Although Grant never said anything in particular and he didn't seem mad, in the light of day my doubts were bigger than ever. I couldn't shake the notion that we'd never talked about how he *felt* about what I'd done, and until we did, things weren't going to get better.

Filled with determination, I turned off the DVD I was watching and looked at him. We'd spent all day together—scratch that—all day in the same house, doing nothing. He looked good sitting in his favorite club chair, mystery novel in hand. He looked so comfortable and relaxed I almost didn't want to ruin it.

"Grant?"

"What's up?"

I hesitated. Did I really want to have this conversation? My heart kicked as I watched Grant turn the page and keep reading without looking up at me. Yeah, we needed this conversation. *I* needed it.

"Did you have a good day?

"Yes, it was good, and you?"

"I'm a bit . . . off." I chewed on my bottom lip, wishing he'd look at me.

"Off?" He finally glanced in my direction.

"Yes." I took a deep breath. "I'm worried about us."

Grant set his book down and gave me his full attention. "Worried?"

"Yes, worried." His one-word answers scraped on my already raw nerves. "We've gone from almost no sex life to a life where we have sex almost every day, but we haven't made love in weeks, and we don't talk."

"We talk."

That's it? We talk? "Okay, we talk, but we don't communicate."

He was silent, his eyes steady as he stared at me. I couldn't see anything behind them. The wall was still there, just like it had been for the last two weeks. So I took another swing at it.

"Grant, you said if I ever had a problem to *talk* to you about it. I'm trying but you have to meet me halfway!"

That got a reaction.

"Damn it, Bethany!" He jumped up from his chair to pace the carpet in front of me. The vein in his temple throbbed, and I saw the emotional wall he'd built around himself finally fall. "I've met you more than halfway. I work my ass off to make sure we have a nice life, and you feel unattractive and unwanted. I forgive you for . . . some pretty extreme things, and give you the attention and structure you obviously need and you're still not happy. What more do you want from me?"

"I want to know how you *feel!*"

He threw his hands up in the air. "Right now I'm pissed off."

We stared at each other for a moment. Fear had a stranglehold on my heart.

"I want to know that you forgive me. That you still love me!"

"Of course, I still love you. If I didn't love you, I wouldn't be here."

"But you're not here. Not completely. Not since . . . since that afternoon in the backyard."

He sighed and ran a hand through his hair. "Talk to me, Grant." I pleaded with him.

"I love you, Bethany. But when I think about you lying to me, I don't like you."

It was a gut punch. A verbal one, but a punch to the gut, nonetheless. My knees gave out and I sank to the sofa, breathless. He didn't like me.

"Bethany, I—"

I put my hand up, cutting him off. I needed a moment. He didn't like me because he thought I lied to him. "I never lied to you."

"Bethany," he shook his head. There was pain and anger and hurt in his gaze and I knew it was for both of us.

"I never lied to you. I never deliberately did anything to hurt to you. I did what I did because it made *me* feel good. It made me feel attractive and sexy and wanted because you were to busy to do it."

"So it's my fault?"

The incredulous hurt on his face made me stop and take a deep breath. Lashing out wasn't the answer. Neither was laying blame.

"No, that's not what I meant." I stood up and went to him. "I'm not blaming you. I love you, and I'm sorry what I did hurt you. That was never my intention. You were busy, and I was lonely. I didn't think."

The anger drained out of Grant at my soft words, but doubt was still there. His voice was quiet but firm when he replied, "There are going to be times when I'm busy, Bethany. How can I know that you won't do it again? Or even go a step further next time?"

"I won't. I promise."

"I don't know that your promise is enough."

My heart tumbled and spots danced before my eyes. He sounded so . . . defeated. As if he didn't have any faith left in me, in *us*. My legs buckled, and I was on my knees in front of him. My hands gripped his and I looked up at him, "I swear I will do anything to prove my love and loyalty to you, Grant. You can't give up on us."

His expression went strangely calm as he looked down at me. "I'm not going to give up on us." He sank to his knees in front of me, and cupped my face in his hand. "Before I met you, I experimented with a few things, dated some kinky women. Including one who was really into sex in public places. It was fun for a while, but then it got to the point where unless we were in danger of getting caught, she couldn't get off. And it worries me to think that you got bit by the same bug, because while it can be fun every now and then, I don't want it to *have* to be that way."

"No, that's not what it was for me." I shook my head. "It wasn't about the risk, it was about being sexy . . . being wanted."

He nodded. "And you get that when I go dominant, don't you?"

"Yes." Heat crept up my neck and I spoke softly. Him getting all commanding and dominant really did it for me. "But I don't want that all the time either. I love *you*, Grant. And for a while it felt like I'd lost you. Not just in the bedroom, but in life. There was no joking around, no movies, no *us* time. I need some time with you when we as a couple can be the main focus."

"I need that too." He traced his thumb lightly over my lips before giving me a soft kiss. When he lifted his head he gazed at me sternly. "No more flashing strangers for you, and more *quality* time for us. I know what you need to stay happy now, and I'm going to give it to you. But in return, you need to trust me completely."

Hope lifted my heavy heart. "I do." I nodded frantically.

"You trust that I know what's best for us, and you'll bow to my wishes?" A dark eyebrow arched over eyes that were starting to shine.

My insides warmed and my juices started to flow south. "Yes, sir."

"And if you misbehave, you will be punished."

Oh, God. Electric excitement flowed through my veins at his words, at the shift in his tone of voice. This was what I needed.

"Yes, sir."

He gathered me in his arms and whispered in my ear. "You are mine, always."

Chapter Twenty-five

Three weeks later we were walking through the park after dinner. Fall was in full swing, the leaves were changing color, and the air at night was getting colder. But in the early evening, it was still warm enough for me to walk around in a sundress and be comfortable.

Things had changed a bit at home. Grant still worked hard, long hours keeping him busier than we would like, but when we were together, we made the time count.

As we strolled along the bike path that surrounded the man-made lake near our home, I thought about how the addition of the submission/domination role-playing to our love life had saved us. I don't know if it was the actual physical aspects of the power exchange—no, I do know. I know it wasn't *just* the physical aspect that helped.

What made Grant's domination of me so damn arousing was the way it made me feel like I was completely and totally his. In my mind, when he went into 'Dom mode' he was telling me exactly how important I was to him, and *that* aroused me more than anything.

Aside from the physical aspects of this new twist, it really opened up our communication. Grant made me talk about everything, there was no room to hold back. And when I spoke, he listened. There was no more wondering about what the other was thinking. It was known. We were both committed, and we knew that to make it work and last forever, we needed to always be able to talk to one another.

And to be able to play with one another.

Grant was the man of the house in every sense of the word, but he treated me like I was his queen. He accepted my submission and my neediness, and gave me respect and boundaries in return. It was a true partnership.

And as an equal partner, I found healthy ways to incorporate my newly developed exhibitionist streak into our lives.

I hugged his arm to me as we as we walked and tried not to grin like an idiot. "Did you know that the digital camera you gave me for my birthday also records movies?"

Yes, I was still pretty limited in my technical knowledge of things, but with the right incentive, I learned fast.

"I'm not surprised. Jason said it did everything." He gave me a suspicious look. "Why?"

My unbound breasts rubbed against his arm, and I told him about the show that I'd taped for him. The one that starred me and my vibrator, and was for his eyes only.

"And where is this movie now?" he asked.

"I emailed it to you. So you have something to watch before you go into your meeting tomorrow."

"You are naughty," he said with a laugh.

"Who me?" I winked at him.

I could see past the shock to the lust glowing in his eyes. My exploits had turned him on too. As much as we both enjoyed him being in charge, we both also enjoyed it when I let a bit of the naughty girl out on my own.

I noticed a lone man sitting against a tree trunk just off the path ahead of us. He was reading a book and ignoring the people passing him by. I glanced at a group of trees close to us and acted on impulse.

I leaned in closer and whispered in his ear, "Please, can I make you come?"

"Oh, you're going to," he said chuckling.

"I want to do it now." In a burst of playful force, I steered him firmly off the path to the shaded area closer to us. I pushed him up against the trunk of the largest tree and pressed my lips to his.

His hands gripped my hips and pulled me close as our mouths meshed and tongues tangled. His heartbeat pounded against my hand as I rubbed against him like a cat in heat, and mine fell in sync with it. Dragging my mouth from his, I nibbled my way up to his ear.

"I want to take your cock into my mouth right now." My hand dropped down his front and cupped him through his shorts. "I'm going to drop to my knees right here in the park and make you come. I'm going to lick, and nibble, and suck you into my mouth, take you deep and let you feel the back of my throat with the head of your cock. Would you like that?"

"There are people here, Bethany." He groaned as if in pain and held me against him. I could feel his cock throbbing as I stroked him through his shorts. "Someone will see."

"Maybe," I whispered. "Maybe not. If we stay quiet, people won't even look over here. It's well shaded, off the path. And anyway, do you really care?" I continued to stroke his cock and let my other hand wander under his T-shirt to his sensitive nipples. Scraping my nails over one and then the other, I kissed him deeply again.

Voices got louder as people got closer, and then faded as they passed us without a hitch. "See," I said. "No one is paying any attention to us."

I slid my body down the front of his and mouthed his cock through his shorts. Grant stifled a groan of pleasure and closed his eyes while letting his hands rest on my head. I opened my eyes and strained to look to my left. There he was, the guy reading under a tree not twenty feet away. Only he wasn't reading anymore. He was watching us.

"Someone is watching, Grant." I slowly pulled his shorts down just past his hips and his ready cock bounced out and hugged his belly. "Look to your right. Can you see him?"

"Umm. Yeah, I see him, just his feet. Give him a show, baby. Show him how much you love to suck me."

My fingers circled the base of his shaft and pulled it away from his belly. I licked up the underside and circled the angry red head with the tip of my tongue. Placing my lips over the top of his cock, I sucked him into my mouth gently. Closing my eyes, I took him deep until he hit the back of my throat and then I slid my mouth back up. I started a slow steady rhythm, one hand cupping his balls and the other stroking in time with my mouth. My pace picked up when I felt his fingers sink deeper into my hair and grip my head firmly. His cock hardened even more and grew thicker in my mouth.

I knew the signs, and it wasn't going to take much more for him to come.

Gripping the base of his cock tightly, I concentrated my sucking on the head. I sucked hard and bobbed my head fast and furious, my tongue teasing the underside with every stroke.

"Arghhh." Grant tried to muffle his groan as I released the base of his cock and took him deep into my throat once again. I felt the throbbing start, and his hands held my head close to him. His pubic bone butted against my nose, and I struggled for breath as his hips pumped a few times, and he shot his load deep into my throat. My mouth filled, and warmth oozed from between my lips and trickled down my chin.

I sat back on my heels and glanced to my left. The stranger was still there, still watching. I smiled at him and wiped the corners of my mouth with my fingertips like a real lady. He smiled back and applauded silently.

Grant's hands gripped my shoulders firmly, and he pulled me to my feet. When he was done kissing me gently, he pulled back and looked at me with a gleam in his eyes.

"Very naughty, Bethany. Now, I must take you home and punish you for such wanton behavior."

Epilogue

I knew everything was truly all right with Grant and me after that walk through the park. Our sex life was pretty adventurous, our *love* life even stronger. I could honestly say that Grant was everything I could ever have asked for, and more than I ever dreamed of.

There was no doubt in my mind he loved me. And I did everything possible to make sure he knew I'd do anything to please him.

Grant still worked too much and I still tested his patience—and his control—every once in a while, with my naughty behavior. But now, when I tested him, it was with the knowledge that he'd bring me back in line, and let me know just where my place in the world was.

Right there with him, at his side, and often on my knees.